NEURAL GHOST

BEYOND THE CIRCUIT REACH

NIHAL SRIVASTAV

LIFE TRULY ENDS THE MOMENT

YOU CHOOSE A LIFE OF COMFORT

Contents

Contents

Preface

In a world where reality is no longer defined by physical boundaries, Kusha finds herself trapped within a digital realm that mirrors her deepest fears and regrets. The journey ahead is one of self-discovery, as the line between the real and the virtual begins to blur, forcing Kusha to confront the ghosts of her past. As she navigates this unstable world, she is not alone. A fragmented team of allies, some more reliable than others, will either guide or deceive her in her fight to break free from the digital prison that holds her captive. In this dystopian world, where glitches and code define the fabric of existence, Kusha's battle is not just against the system, but also within herself. The scars of a traumatic breakup, the ghosts of a painful childhood, and the remnants of her shattered self-esteem haunt every corner of her mind. Her journey is as much about survival as it is about healine With each chapter, Kusha will learn that to escape, she must first understand the intricacies of her own soul and confront the unresolved past that still governs her actions in the present.

In a world as deadly as walking on a sword, will she find redemption, or will she be consumed by the system and her own ghosts?

This is a story of strength and vulnerability, where the struggle is not only for survival but for self-realization in a world that no longer feels like home.

1

The Unseen Gate

The storm wasn't outside—it was inside her. Kusha sat cross-legged on her narrow cot, staring at the faint glow of her phone screen. The name still hovered there, a shadow she couldn't erase. Rohan. Months had passed since their breakup, but the weight of it still clung to her like wet clothes. Some nights, she thought she'd finally drowned the memories. Other nights, like tonight, they surged back in waves, pulling her under. Her hand hovered over the notification, her thumb trembling. She deleted the call, but it didn't help. The damage was done. Rohan had clawed his way back into her mind, and now the past played out in cruel flashes: the arguments, his cold silence, the way he walked away when she needed him the most. Kusha rubbed her temples, trying to steady her breathing. "Move on, Kusha," she whispered, but even as she said it, she knew it wasn't that simple. Moving on meant forgetting, and forgetting felt impossible. The small room around her offered no comfort. The walls were bare except for a single cracked mirror, and the ceiling fan creaked with every turn. Outside, the faint hum of crickets and rustling leaves filled the night air, but even that seemed distant, like the world itself was holding its breath. She looked at her reflection in the mirror. The woman staring back at her was tired—dark circles under her eyes, hair unkempt, shoulders slumped as if carrying a weight too heavy to bear. For a moment, the reflection seemed to flicker, her face distorting into something unfamiliar. Kusha blinked, her heart skipping a beat. The reflection returned to normal, but the unease lingered. She shook her head and turned away. "Just tired," she muttered. "That's all." The power went out just after midnight. Kusha had been lying in bed, staring at the ceiling, when the room plunged into darkness. The sudden silence was deafening. No fan. No buzzing lightbulb. Even the crickets outside seemed to fall quiet. She sat up, her chest tightening. The darkness felt alive, pressing against her like a suffocating weight. Then she saw it—the glow. A faint blue light seeped through the cracks of her bedroom door. It pulsed rhythmically, like a heartbeat. Kusha froze, her mind racing. Was someone in the house? Her parents were away visiting relatives, and she was supposed to be alone. Her first instinct was to stay put, to lock the door and wait for the glow to disappear. But something about it drew her in, a strange pull she couldn't explain. It wasn't fear—it was curiosity. She slid out of bed, her bare feet touching the cold wooden floor. The boards creaked under her weight as she approached the door. With trembling hands, she turned the knob and peeked into the hallway. The glow was coming from the study room at the end of the hall. The study room hadn't been used in years. It was where her father used to work, back when he was still alive. Since his death, it had become a storage space, filled with dusty books and old furniture no one cared to sort through. Kusha's pulse quickened as she stepped inside. The air was colder here, carrying the faint smell of damp wood and mildew. But it was the source of the light that held her attention. An old desktop computer sat on the desk in the corner, its screen glowing with the same blue light she'd seen through her door. Kusha frowned. She didn't remember seeing the computer there before. She approached cautiously, her eyes fixed on the screen. Strange symbols and shifting patterns moved across it, like a language she couldn't understand. For a moment, she thought about turning back, about shutting the door and pretending she hadn't seen anything. But the symbols seemed to draw her in, hypnotizing her. Suddenly, the screen went blank. Kusha froze. Then, words began to appear, one letter at a time. "DO YOU WISH TO LEAVE IT BEHIND?" Her heart pounded in her chest. She didn't understand what it meant, but the question sent a chill down her spine. "Leave what behind?" she whispered, her voice barely audible. The screen flickered, and the question appeared again, bolder this time: "DO YOU WISH TO LEAVE IT BEHIND?" Kusha hesitated. Her fingers hovered over the keyboard, trembling. Her mind raced with possibilities. Was this some kind of prank? A virus? Or something else entirely? Before she could think it through, her hands moved on their own. Her fingers brushed the keys, typing out a single word. "Yes." The moment she pressed enter, the screen exploded with light. It wasn't a physical explosion—there was no sound, no force—but the light consumed everything. The room around her dissolved into fragments, the walls and furniture breaking apart into pixels and streaks of color. Kusha felt herself falling, though her body remained still. She tried to scream, but no sound came out. When the light faded, she wasn't in her house anymore. The ground beneath her was cold and metallic, and the air was thick with a strange hum. She staggered to her feet, her heart racing as she took in her surroundings.

The world around her was unlike anything she had ever seen. The sky was an infinite expanse of black, dotted with glowing grids and flickering lights. The ground stretched out in all directions, a smooth metallic surface that seemed to hum beneath her feet. In the distance, a massive tower loomed, its structure pulsating with the same blue glow that had consumed her. Kusha took a hesitant step forward, her footsteps echoing unnaturally. She didn't know where she was or how she had gotten here, but one thing was clear—this place was not meant to exist. A voice broke the silence, soft and melodic, yet undeniably eerie. "Welcome, Kusha. You've finally arrived."

2

The Gates of Judgment

Kusha's eyes burned as she blinked against the harsh light that filled her vision. For a moment, she couldn't tell if she was dreaming or awake. The moment she had crossed into this new, bewildering place, she had been struck by a sense of wrongness. She tried to calm her breath, but the air felt thin, like she was suffocating on the weight of a thousand unspoken thoughts. She reached out, her hand trembling, and touched the cold, smooth surface beneath her feet. It was hard, metallic, almost as if the ground were made of liquid silver—so reflective that it mirrored her own startled expression, distorting her features into something alien. But that wasn't the most unsettling thing. The most unsettling thing was how quiet it was. There was no sound here. No wind, no hum of electricity, no birds or insects. Only silence. Silence that filled her ears and crawled under her skin like a living thing. "Welcome, Kusha. You've finally arrived." The voice that boomed in her mind felt like it had been there forever, waiting for her to notice it. It was calm but distant, reverberating through the empty space like a thunderclap in a vast, hollow cavern. Kusha's heart skipped a beat. Her eyes darted around, seeking the source of the voice, but she saw nothing. The space was completely empty. "Who are you?" Kusha demanded, her voice echoing louder than she had intended. It felt strange, as if the voice wasn't just in the air but in her mind—deep, all-consuming. "Where am I?" "This is the Nexus, Kusha. The heart of the digital world. The place where your past, present, and future converge." Kusha staggered back, her mind struggling to process the words. Nexus? Digital world? The words felt cold, unfamiliar, and utterly nonsensical. Her past? Present? Future? What did that even mean in this strange, unyielding place? Her head spun as she tried to steady herself. She couldn't focus. Nothing here made sense. How did she even get here? The last thing she remembered was sitting at her computer, trying to block out the haunting thoughts of her past, of Rohan, of everything that had broken her. But now... she was here. The voice continued, its tone unreadable, yet it sent a chill running through her spine. "You were chosen, Kusha. The world you once knew is no longer yours. You must face the trials ahead—or remain lost forever." Kusha's thoughts spiraled in a dark spiral of confusion. Chosen? Lost forever? Was this some sort of punishment? Was this a twisted dream from which she couldn't wake? She felt the weight of her memories pressing down on her, each one more painful than the last. "I don't belong here," she muttered under her breath. But deep inside, she knew that wasn't true. She was here, wasn't she? And if she was here, there had to be a reason. Before she could even think about the consequences, the world around her began to shift. The metallic ground rippled, like liquid silver disturbed by an invisible force. The sky darkened, a deep, shifting black that stretched on without end. A massive shape appeared before her, its form shifting in the ever-changing landscape—like the outline of a gate, but not quite real. It was made of floating pixels, each one a piece of data that flickered in and out of existence. It resembled an ancient, glowing doorway, though its edges warped and fractured in unpredictable patterns, as if the very fabric of reality was being eaten away. The voice spoke again, now more urgent. "Through this gate lies your first trial. The path to your redemption begins now." Kusha's legs felt like they were made of stone. Her thoughts were a storm of doubt and fear. She didn't know what awaited her on the other side of that gate, but something in her gut told her that stepping through it would mean losing even more of herself. But she couldn't stop now, could she? She had no choice. She had to move forward. With a shaky breath, Kusha forced herself to step toward the gate. The moment her foot touched the threshold, the pixels shifted and shimmered, distorting in waves as though the very air around her was alive. The gate flickered and then—disappeared. She blinked, momentarily blinded by the light that flooded her vision. When the light cleared, she found herself in a new place—a narrow, suffocating corridor. It was dark, the walls closing in on her as though they were alive, watching, breathing. The air felt dense, almost oppressive, with a tangible weight that pressed down on her chest. There was something wrong here. It was a place that seemed to exist between spaces, caught in a loop of uncertainty and fear. She walked, every step echoing loudly in the stillness. The passage stretched on, and for a moment, she wondered if it would ever end. Would she be walking forever, trapped in this inescapable labyrinth? Then she saw him. A figure stood motionless ahead of her, his eyes locked onto hers with an unsettling intensity. He was no older than 18, with messy brown hair falling into his eyes and a look of weariness that seemed to stretch beyond his years. His clothes were torn, stained with digital remnants of a world long destroyed. Kusha took a hesitant step forward, her heart thudding in her chest. "Who are you?" she asked, her voice barely above a whisper. The boy didn't respond immediately. He simply stared at her, his expression unreadable, like he was trying to figure her out, or perhaps deciding if she was worth his time. "You don't belong here," he finally said, his voice rough, almost ragged. "This place... it changes people. If you stay too long, you'll lose yourself. If you want to survive, you need to leave now." Kusha shook her head, a bitter laugh escaping her lips. "I can't leave. I have to face whatever this is. This is my only chance to... to fix things." The boy's eyes softened for a moment, and for the first time, she saw the exhaustion beneath his fear. He stepped closer, the digital world around them warping with his movements, as if the very space bent to his will. "You don't understand," he said, his voice quieter now. "You think this world is about fixing things, but it's not. It's about survival. And if you want to survive, you need to trust me." Kusha was silent for a moment, considering his words. Trust him? How could she trust anyone here? Her memories were already shattered, her mind unraveling in ways she couldn't understand. "I can't do this alone," she whispered, almost to herself. The boy nodded, his gaze steady. "Then let me help you. My name is Jerry." Her heart skipped a beat at the sound of his name, but she didn't question it. There was something in his eyes, some flicker of honesty, that made her take a step closer. "Okay," Kusha said, her voice trembling but resolute. "I'll follow you."

3

The Trial of the Digital Maze

Kusha's mind raced as she followed Jerry deeper into the labyrinth of the digital world. Every step seemed to echo in the unnerving silence that surrounded them. The walls, made of a flickering web of binary code, shimmered in and out of existence, as if they were unstable, ready to collapse at any moment. Jerry moved with purpose, his eyes scanning the shifting patterns of light and shadow. He appeared at ease, even though Kusha could feel the tension in the air growing heavier with every passing second. "Where are we going?" Kusha's voice trembled, though she hated how weak it sounded. "Somewhere safe," Jerry said without looking back. "Trust me. We need to get through this maze first." Kusha didn't question him. At least not right away. What else could she do in this strange, terrifying world? She didn't know the rules, and she didn't understand the purpose of her being here, but she did know one thing: she couldn't face whatever awaited her alone. Suddenly, the space around them warped again. The binary code that had once looked like walls turned into an endless maze, each corridor twisting in impossible angles. The floor beneath their feet was slick with a strange energy, sending shocks of coldness up Kusha's spine. "This isn't normal," Kusha whispered. Jerry stopped, his expression hardening as he turned to face her. "I know," he said quietly. "But it's the only way forward. This place is a test. It will try to break you down. It will exploit every weakness. If you don't face your fears, you won't make it." Kusha swallowed hard. "I don't even know what my fear is." "You will," Jerry said with a grim smile. "And you'll have to face it. Everyone does." Before Kusha could respond, a loud, grinding sound echoed through the maze. The walls shifted violently, and a new path opened up in front of them. It was dark, almost suffocating, and there was something wrong about it. Kusha could feel it deep in her bones. "Stay close," Jerry warned, his voice now low and tense. Kusha nodded, her heart pounding in her chest. She had no choice but to trust him. With every step, the fear inside her grew stronger, but she fought to keep it under control. She had no idea what was coming next, but she wasn't about to lose herself here. The maze seemed endless, its corridors stretching on into infinity. The air grew colder, and the walls began to close in, each step more oppressive than the last. As they walked deeper into the labyrinth, Kusha felt a strange sensation creeping up her spine. It was as though something—or someone—was watching her. Suddenly, the ground beneath their feet cracked open with a violent jolt. Kusha gasped as she found herself falling, her body twisting uncontrollably through the void. There was no ground, no walls, just darkness rushing at her from every direction. The fall seemed to stretch on forever, her body weightless, lost in the void. She screamed out, but her voice was swallowed by the silence, as if she didn't even exist anymore. It was the worst sensation Kusha had ever felt—the sensation of being utterly alone, falling endlessly into nothingness. Just when she thought she couldn't take it anymore, a light appeared below her—a soft, glowing pulse in the distance. She reached for it, desperate to grasp hold of something, anything, that would stop her descent. Her body hit the ground with a painful thud, and she gasped, the air knocked out of her lungs. She struggled to breathe, but the light was still there, a soft beacon in the midst of the overwhelming darkness. Kusha forced herself to stand, her legs shaking beneath her. She was disoriented, but she couldn't afford to stay down. She had to keep moving. Ahead of her, Jerry appeared, his face grim but determined. "You made it," he said, offering her a hand. "But this is just the beginning." Kusha took his hand, trying to steady herself. "What was that? Why did we fall?" "It's the trial," Jerry explained, his voice steady. "The digital maze tests you. It tries to break you mentally and physically. But you have to push through. The deeper you go, the harder it becomes. The fear... it's all real. You just have to face it." Kusha's heart was still pounding in her chest. She didn't know what to make of the trial, but she knew she couldn't afford to lose herself here. She had to keep going. For herself. For everything she had left to prove. They continued through the maze, each step more difficult than the last. The walls closed in tighter, the air grew colder, and every corner they turned felt more claustrophobic. The maze seemed to warp around them, shifting with every thought and feeling. The more Kusha fought her fear, the stronger the maze pushed back. As they moved deeper, Kusha felt the weight of her past growing heavier. The darkness seemed to feed on her memories, each step pulling her deeper into the abyss of her own regrets. The ground beneath her feet became unstable, and she could hear voices—faint whispers at first, then growing louder, echoing in the dark. "Kusha…" The voice was haunting, familiar. "You can't outrun your past." She froze, her blood running cold. The voice was Rohan's. Her ex. The man who had broken her heart. "No…" Kusha muttered, shaking her head. "This isn't real." But the voice grew louder, more insistent. "You'll never escape the guilt. You'll never escape the pain." The walls around her seemed to close in tighter, the darkness pressing down on her like a weight. Kusha tried to push through, but the pressure was too much. She couldn't breathe. She couldn't escape the suffocating memory of her past, of Rohan's betrayal, of everything she had lost. "Kusha!" Jerry's voice cut through the haze of her thoughts. "Don't let it control you! Face it! You have to fight it!" Kusha's eyes snapped open. The maze, the voices—it was all an illusion, a test. She realized then that the only way out was to confront her fears, to face what she had been running from for so long. She took a deep breath, squaring her shoulders. "I won't let you win," she whispered, her voice firm. With newfound strength, Kusha pressed forward. The maze shifted again, the walls giving way to a new path. The voices faded, and for the first time, Kusha felt a glimmer of hope. She wasn't just fighting for survival anymore—she was fighting for herself. And she would not lose. I can expand the chapter further, delving deeper into Kusha's emotional turmoil, adding more description and psychological depth.

4
Fragments of Lost

The eerie hum of the maze surrounded Kusha and Jerry as they ventured deeper into the labyrinthine world. Every corner they turned revealed the same cold metallic walls, flickering lights casting ominous shadows. The deeper they went, the more oppressive the atmosphere became. It felt as though the maze itself was alive, watching them, waiting for them to make a mistake. Kusha's heartbeat quickened with every step, the weight of her thoughts pressing heavily on her chest. The maze wasn't just a physical challenge—it was a test of her mind, her soul. And the further they pushed forward, the more it began to feel like a confrontation with the very demons she had spent years trying to bury. "I think we're getting closer," Jerry muttered, his voice barely audible over the strange humming sound that seemed to come from everywhere and nowhere at once. "Stay sharp." Kusha nodded without saying a word, her thoughts far away. She couldn't stop thinking about what had happened in the previous trial. The memories—so vivid, so raw—had come flooding back, tearing open wounds she had spent a lifetime trying to close. She thought she had outrun them, that the trauma of her childhood had been buried under layers of time, but the maze had found a way to dig it all back up. Every corner, every step she took felt like a journey deeper into the darkness of her past. As they moved, Kusha's gaze flickered to Jerry, who walked beside her, his posture tense and alert. His eyes were scanning every shadow, every flicker of light. She was grateful for him, more than she could express. But even with his presence, she couldn't escape the gnawing feeling that something was following them. Something unseen. A sudden cry pierced the air—soft, distant, but unmistakable. Kusha froze. The voice was faint at first, but as the seconds ticked by, it grew louder, more distinct. She could feel it in her bones, a resonance that shook her to the core. It was a voice she recognized. A voice from the past. The voice of a younger Kusha. Her pulse spiked, and her legs felt like lead. She wanted to run, to close her ears, to escape it—but she couldn't. The voice called her name. "Kusha..." The sound of it, so familiar, sent a shiver down her spine. It was a cry of pain, of helplessness, of abandonment. It was the voice of the child she had once been, the girl who had been left behind, the girl who had been forgotten. The voice that had haunted her dreams. "No," she whispered to herself. "No, it's not real. It's just this place—this damn maze." But deep down, she knew it wasn't just the maze. It was her. The maze was pulling at her deepest, most fragile parts, forcing her to confront the very things she had buried beneath years of hurt and anger. The voice came again, louder this time, more urgent. "Kusha... help me..." She squeezed her eyes shut, fighting the flood of memories. She wanted to tell herself it was just a trick, just an illusion. But the voice was too real. It was too painful. Jerry turned to her, his face serious. "Stay with me. Don't let it get to you." But Kusha could feel herself slipping. The walls of the maze began to close in on her. The cry echoed in her ears, growing louder, more insistent. The distorted image of her mother's face appeared in her mind, cold and distant, accusing her of everything that had gone wrong in her life. Her mother's abandonment, her endless emotional needs that had never been met—Kusha had been left to fend for herself, to grow up in a world of emotional isolation. "You left me," the voice whispered, distorted now, the tone dripping with venom. "You abandoned me, just like everyone else." Kusha's breath caught in her throat, and for a moment, she could see the figure of her mother standing before her. The cruel smile, the eyes that never seemed to care. It was the same look she had seen when she was a child, the same rejection she had felt when her mother had chosen her father's side over her. Kusha's chest tightened as the pain of that betrayal rushed back. The feeling of being unwanted, unworthy, had followed her into adulthood, leaving scars that no amount of time could heal. The walls seemed to warp around her, the ground beneath her feet shifting, and she stumbled forward, clutching her head in a desperate attempt to block out the images. The walls were no longer cold and metallic; they were like the walls of her childhood home, suffocating, oppressive. The air felt thick with regret and sadness, a weight she could hardly bear. "Please," Kusha whispered, her voice barely audible. "Please stop..." But the voices wouldn't stop. They circled around her, growing louder, echoing in her ears. She couldn't escape. Her mind was spinning out of control. The digital world around her warped into the very real, very painful memories of her childhood. The scars she had carried for years were laid bare before her eyes, and she couldn't run from them. She was trapped, not just in the maze, but in the past she had tried so hard to forget. "Kusha..." The voice was right behind her now. Her legs gave way, and she collapsed to the floor, her head spinning, her body trembling. "I'm sorry... I'm sorry... I didn't mean to..." Her words were drowned out by the rising cacophony of voices. The cruel laughter of the girl she once was, the desperate cries of a child who had been abandoned. Kusha felt herself being torn apart, caught between the past and the present. "No..." she whispered, shaking her head. "I'm not that girl anymore. I'm not her..." The voice faltered, and the figure of her mother seemed to flicker, as if the illusion was breaking down. Kusha's chest heaved with every ragged breath. She forced herself to look up, to meet the distorted figure before her. "You're not real," she spat, her voice stronger now, more certain. "I'm not the broken girl I was. I've moved on. I've survived." The illusion wavered, flickering like a bad signal on a screen, and then it vanished. The weight that had pressed down on her chest seemed to lift, and the walls of the maze returned to their cold, metallic form. The oppressive atmosphere lightened, and the path ahead grew clearer. Jerry's steady hand pulled her to her feet, and she looked up at him, her eyes full of gratitude and something more—strength, perhaps. "You did it," he said quietly, his voice calm but filled with pride. Kusha swallowed hard, her heart still racing. "I don't know how... but I know I have to let go." The words hung in the air between them, heavy with meaning. She wasn't the girl who had been abandoned anymore. She was no longer the scared child trapped in her own past. "You're not alone," Jerry said gently, as though reading her thoughts. "You've got me." Kusha nodded, the weight of her past still lingering but no longer controlling her. "I'm not alone," she repeated. "And I'm not that girl anymore." With renewed determination, she took a step forward. The maze was still dangerous, still filled with traps and illusions, but for the first time, Kusha felt ready to face whatever it threw her way. She wasn't running from her past anymore. She was moving forward And with Jerry by her side, she knew she could face whatever was to come.

5

The Collapse Begins

Kusha felt the weight of her own emotions pressing down on her with every step she took. The path ahead seemed clear now, but the darkness that still lingered within her made the world around her feel like a constant battle. She was no longer haunted by the child she used to be, but the scars from her past still threatened to resurface at every turn. Jerry walked beside her, a steady presence, his gaze scanning the horizon, never leaving her side. "We need to keep moving," he said, his voice firm. "The further we go, the closer we get to the truth." Kusha nodded, her mind still reeling from the vision of her mother. But there was no time to dwell. The maze, as dangerous and disorienting as it was, had to be navigated. The further they ventured, the more Kusha realized that every step forward felt like a step into the unknown—a place where the boundaries between reality and illusion blurred. "We can do this," she whispered to herself. She wasn't sure if it was for her own comfort or if she was trying to reassure Jerry, but it felt like a necessary mantra. They had come so far, but she knew it wasn't going to be easy. It wasn't just the maze they had to conquer—it was the instability of the digital world, the glitches, the threats of the entities that resided within it. The first signs of instability appeared in the form of shifting patterns on the walls. The once-steady hum began to distort, echoing like a broken soundwave. Kusha could feel the ground trembling beneath her feet, as though the very foundation of the world was beginning to collapse. "Something's wrong," Kusha said, her voice tense. Jerry looked around, his brow furrowed. "The maze... it's changing. It wasn't like this before." Before Kusha could respond, the ground beneath them cracked open, and the walls shifted, collapsing into a void of nothingness. The hum of the maze grew louder, more intense, like a storm was gathering inside the very digital fabric of the world. Kusha's heart raced. "What's happening?" A low, mechanical voice echoed from the walls. "System failure. Reconfiguration in progress." "What does that mean?" Jerry asked, his eyes scanning the now-dark surroundings. "It means we're running out of time," Kusha said. "We need to find the core. Now." The maze around them began to distort further, the path ahead twisting and warping. What had once been a straight passage now curved and split into multiple directions. Kusha could see the glitching zones, dark spots where reality seemed to break down completely. Time, too, seemed to bend. The clock on Kusha's wrist flickered, showing moments in the past—memories from her childhood, brief flashes of faces, and moments she had tried to forget. The deeper they went, the more oppressive the atmosphere became. Kusha could feel herself losing grip on reality as she was sucked back into her mind, into the memories she had tried so hard to bury. The path ahead was no longer just a physical challenge—it was a race against time and her own mind. Suddenly, a flash of movement caught her eye. It was a shadow—a figure, flickering in and out of view. Kusha's breath caught in her throat, her pulse spiking. The figure was barely visible, but she knew it wasn't human. The figure was something else—something that had no place in this digital world. "Did you see that?" she asked, her voice shaky. Jerry looked ahead. "I saw it. But whatever it is, we need to move." The shadow moved again, faster this time, crossing the corridor and vanishing into the glitching darkness. Kusha's heart pounded as the realization hit her—the maze was not just a trap for her physical body. It was a reflection of her mind, of the brokenness she carried. And whatever these shadows were, they were connected to the forces trying to break her apart. Without warning, the ground shook violently, and the path ahead split open, revealing a chasm that seemed to stretch into infinity. Kusha staggered back, nearly losing her balance. A loud, unearthly sound filled the air, something between a scream and a mechanical whine. "Look!" Jerry shouted, pointing towards the center of the chasm. A glowing red light appeared, pulsing like a heartbeat. It was the core—the center of the system, the place where everything began. It was the key to both the maze's destruction and its salvation. "We need to reach it!" Kusha said, determination flooding her veins. This was it—the moment she had been waiting for. The core was where the answers lay. It was the source of the maze's power, and if they could access it, they could control the outcome. But the closer they got, the more chaotic the environment became. The shadows surged again, this time forming into more distinct shapes. They were figures, not quite human, but not entirely digital either. Their faces were hidden behind masks of static, their movements jerky, as if they were glitching in and out of existence. Kusha gripped Jerry's arm. "We can't stop now. We have to get to the core, no matter what." They began to run, their steps echoing in the vast, empty space. The ground beneath them fractured, each step making the environment around them feel more unstable. The shadows followed, their eerie cries filling the air, drowning out everything else. The further they moved, the more the maze collapsed around them, the walls breaking apart like shattered glass. The core pulsed in the distance, a beacon of red light, growing larger with every step they took. But as they neared it, a massive figure emerged from the shadows—a towering entity made of pure digital static. It was The Architect, his form flickering in and out of reality like a broken transmission. "Stop!" The Architect's voice echoed, cold and commanding. "You cannot reach the core. This system will not allow it." Kusha's pulse quickened. "We don't need your permission." With a fierce push, she and Jerry ran forward, determined to reach the core. The ground trembled violently beneath them as the digital world began to unravel. The Architect's form expanded, reaching toward them with long, spindly limbs, his fingers crackling with electricity. "We are not your prisoners," Kusha shouted, her voice rising above the noise. "We are the ones who will decide how this ends." The Architect's eyes—if they could be called eyes—glowed with a malevolent intensity. "Foolish girl. You cannot escape. This world is mine." Kusha's hand shot out, her fingers brushing the glowing core. A surge of energy flooded through her, and the world around her exploded in a burst of light. Time slowed, the digital landscape collapsing in on itself as the power of the core responded to her touch. This was it. The collapse had begun, and there was no going back now.

6
Breaking the Chains

The world around Kusha dissolved into a chaotic swirl of colors, glitching shapes, and distorted sounds. Her body felt weightless, like she was floating through an endless void. The core's energy had coursed through her, filling her with an overwhelming power that surged through her veins. But the price was high—the more she resisted the pull of the maze, the more the system fought back. Kusha could hear the distant cries of the shadows, their voices like nails scraping against metal, their presence like an ever-encroaching nightmare. They weren't just trying to capture her—they were trying to erase her. Her memories. Her existence. But Kusha wasn't about to let that happen. She could see Jerry beside her, his face tense, eyes wide with the same fear she had. But there was something else too—something that flickered behind his gaze, like a glimmer of understanding. Whatever this core was, whatever it had done to her, it had opened something deep inside Kusha—something primal. "We need to get out of here," she gasped, her voice breaking through the static-filled air. Jerry nodded, but before they could move, the ground beneath them shattered, breaking apart like glass.

A massive hand made of swirling data shot up from the depths, its fingers curling around them. The force was immense, pulling them downward. Kusha's heart raced. She reached out, trying to grab hold of anything stable. But there was nothing—only the pull of the void. The shadows circled them, growing closer, their forms more distinct now, more threatening. "No!" Kusha screamed, her hand stretched out toward Jerry, their fingers barely touching. The world seemed to stretch between them as the hand dragged them into the darkness. But then, something inside Kusha shifted. With every ounce of willpower she could summon, she pushed back against the pull, focusing all her energy on breaking free. The shadows screeched in agony as Kusha unleashed a wave of raw force. The core's power surged through her like a hurricane, her body crackling with energy as she channeled everything into one final push. The hand faltered, its grip loosening as Kusha's power grew. She heard Jerry's voice—a quiet, breathless whisper—"Kusha..." And then, the world shattered. The digital space around them exploded into a flood of light, disintegrating into nothingness. The shadows vanished, their presence lost in the chaos. The core, its once-gleaming surface, cracked and splintered, emitting a final, deafening scream as it too was consumed by the energy. Kusha and Jerry plummeted through the collapsing world, falling through endless layers of data until everything went dark. --- When Kusha awoke, it wasn't the familiar hum of the digital world that greeted her—it was silence. The space she found herself in was unlike anything she had experienced before. It wasn't part of the maze, nor was it a place she recognized. The walls were made of shifting patterns of light and shadow, as if the world itself was breathing. Kusha slowly pushed herself to her feet, her mind foggy but clear enough to understand that something had changed. She was no longer in the digital labyrinth. She was somewhere else—somewhere beyond the boundaries of the system. She turned to see Jerry beside her, equally disoriented but alive. "Kusha," he said, his voice strained. "What just happened?" "I—" Kusha's words faltered as she looked around, trying to make sense of her surroundings. "I think we're out. Out of the maze." "But how?" Jerry asked, his eyes wide with disbelief. "We were supposed to be trapped." "I don't know," Kusha admitted, shaking her head. "But whatever we did, it broke the system. We should be dead. We should have been erased." But the silence around them remained unbroken, and for the first time in what felt like forever, Kusha dared to hope. The digital world had collapsed, but something new was beginning to emerge in its place. Something different. She could feel it in the air—the energy that thrummed beneath her skin, the knowledge that they had unlocked something beyond the confines of the system. But at the same time, Kusha knew the danger was far from over. The Architect, The Anomaly, the digital ghosts—they were still out there, waiting, and they weren't going to let go so easily. There were forces in motion that Kusha could barely comprehend, forces that wanted to control the fate of everyone trapped within the system. And as she stared out into the unknown, Kusha understood that the journey wasn't over yet. They had just taken the first step into a new world—a world where the rules were different, where nothing could be trusted, and where every choice could lead to destruction. But this time, Kusha was ready to fight. "We can't stop now," she said, turning to Jerry. "We've come this far. We're not giving up." Jerry nodded, his expression hardening with resolve. "I'm with you. Wherever this takes us." Together, they stepped forward, leaving the broken pieces of the past behind. The future lay ahead, uncertain and terrifying, but Kusha wasn't afraid anymore. She was ready to face whatever came next.

25

7
The Ghosts Within

Kusha's footsteps echoed in the eerie silence that stretched before them. The world they had entered was unlike anything she had imagined. It wasn't the familiar chaos of the digital maze, nor was it the soothing nothingness of being trapped in a void. Instead, it was a place between worlds—an in-between space where reality and the unknown blended into one. She felt a strange energy hum beneath her feet, a pulse that seemed to come from the very fabric of this new world. It wasn't quite physical, nor entirely digital. It was a presence that stretched across dimensions, something beyond comprehension. Beside her, Jerry's expression was a mixture of awe and fear, his eyes scanning their surroundings nervously. "What is this place?" Jerry asked, his voice low. "I don't know," Kusha replied, her eyes narrowed as she took in their surroundings. The air was thick with an almost tangible tension, and the walls—if they could even be called walls—seemed to warp and shimmer, like reflections in a shattered mirror. At times, it felt like the space around them was bending and shifting, as if it were alive. Before Kusha could say anything else, she felt a chill run down her spine.

A presence, one that she couldn't see, but could sense, lingered at the edge of her perception. It wasn't just the space that was alive—it was something within it. Something watching. Suddenly, a voice cut through the air, sending a jolt of fear through her body. "You've made it this far, Kusha." The voice was cold, ethereal, and yet it felt familiar. A memory, distant yet sharp, flickered in Kusha's mind. "Who's there?" she demanded, her tone hardening. "I am the Witness," the voice responded, its tone echoing through the empty space. It was distant yet close at the same time, like a whisper in her ear. "I have seen all who have passed through here... and I have seen you." Kusha's breath caught in her throat as she looked around frantically, searching for the source of the voice. But there was no one. The space remained still and silent. "Witness?" she muttered, trying to place the name. "Who are you?" "I am nothing and everything," the voice replied cryptically. "I have watched the cycle repeat over and over. The ones who come, the ones who go. The broken and the whole. You are both, Kusha." Kusha felt a shiver of unease at the words. She could sense that this being, the Witness, knew far more than she did—about the maze, about the core, and about her. "What do you want from me?" Kusha demanded. The voice lingered, and for a moment, there was silence. Then, the voice spoke again, its words soft but filled with an unsettling weight. "You are here because you chose to be. The path you walk is not one of destiny, but of choice. You have the power to change everything." Jerry, who had been standing beside Kusha, stepped forward, his face drawn with confusion. "What does that mean? Change everything?" "The system," the Witness explained, "is collapsing. You have torn a hole in the fabric of reality, Kusha. The Architect's reign is weakening, and the Anomaly grows stronger. This place, this in-between world, is the key." Kusha felt a flicker of realization spark within her. The Witness was telling the truth. They hadn't just escaped. They had entered something much bigger than they realized—a space that was neither entirely part of the digital world nor completely outside it. It was the space where the system's boundaries broke, where the past and future converged. "So, what now?" Kusha asked, her voice steady despite the chaos swirling inside her. "You must choose," the Witness said, its voice now tinged with a sense of finality. "Will you continue down the path of destruction and chaos, or will you seek to rebuild what has been shattered?" Kusha felt the weight of the decision press down on her. Everything they had been through—the maze, the core, the struggle against The Architect and The Anomaly—it had all led her here. This was the moment of truth. The choice was hers. "We need to rebuild," Kusha said, her voice firm with resolve. "We've seen what destruction looks like. I don't want to be a part of it." The Witness was silent for a long time, its presence looming over them. Then, finally, it spoke again. "Very well. But remember this, Kusha: Not all who enter this place can leave. You will have to face the ghosts of your past, the ones who haunt this world. They will test you, and they will not be merciful." Before Kusha could respond, the space around them began to shift. The walls flickered, and the air grew thick with a presence that seemed to press against her very being. The shadows that had been lingering in the background now solidified into forms. Figures, ghostly and half-formed, drifted through the shifting space, their eyes glowing with an eerie light. They were the manifestations of all those who had been lost in the system—trapped, forgotten, and now, awakened by the collapse of the world.

Kusha's heart pounded in her chest. These weren't just ghosts. They were the remnants of the minds that had once been part of the system—trapped souls, now seeking freedom, but also hungry for revenge. "We must leave," Jerry whispered urgently, grabbing Kusha's arm. "This place is a trap." But Kusha stood her ground, her eyes locked on the approaching figures. She had come this far, and she wasn't going to back down now. "I'm not afraid of them," she said, her voice steady despite the fear gnawing at her insides. "I've faced worse." But as the ghosts closed in, their whispers filling the air like a chorus of tormented souls, Kusha realized one thing—she wasn't just fighting for herself anymore. She was fighting for everyone who had been lost, for everyone who had been erased by the system. And with that thought, she steeled herself for the battle ahead.

8
The Battle for Control

The air around Kusha crackled with tension. The ghosts that surrounded her were not mere figments of the digital world; they were something far more terrifying. Their forms flickered in and out of reality, their eyes glowing with an eerie light that seemed to pierce through her very soul. As Kusha stood her ground, she could feel their presence pressing against her, suffocating her with a sense of dread. The weight of their combined misery was overwhelming, and for a moment, she wondered if she had made a mistake in choosing to face them. "We need to get out of here," Jerry urged, his voice trembling with fear. He looked around, his eyes wide with panic. "This place... it's a death trap." But Kusha didn't flinch. She couldn't. Not now. Not when they had come so far. The ghosts—they weren't just enemies. They were part of the system. Part of the world Kusha had come to destroy. And if she was ever going to rebuild it, she had to face them. "No," Kusha said firmly, her voice unwavering. "We're not running. We're fighting." Jerry opened his mouth to protest, but before he could say anything, the first of the ghosts lunged forward with a screech, its form a twisted, contorted version of a human.

Its mouth opened impossibly wide, emitting a guttural growl that sent a chill down Kusha's spine. She could feel its hunger, its anger, and its desperation to escape. Without thinking, Kusha reached for the energy she had learned to tap into, the power that had sustained her through the trials of the digital world. It surged through her like a river, her mind clearing as she focused on the task ahead. "Stay close," Kusha said to Jerry, her voice steady as she raised her hand. A pulse of energy shot out from her fingertips, colliding with the ghost's twisted form. It screamed in agony, its body disintegrating into a cloud of data fragments before it vanished. But there were more. So many more. The other ghosts advanced, their forms shifting and warping with each step. Some were humanoid, others less recognizable—faceless entities with long, gnarled limbs that seemed to stretch out toward Kusha and Jerry, their eyes glowing with malice. Kusha felt the strain of the battle beginning to wear on her. Each blast of energy she fired took a toll on her strength, and she could feel her body growing weaker with each passing moment. But she couldn't stop. She couldn't give in. "Jerry!" she shouted, her voice sharp with urgency. "You have to help me!" Jerry hesitated for a moment, his fear evident in his eyes. But then, as if driven by some deep instinct, he stepped forward. With a swift motion, he raised his hands and conjured a blast of energy. It wasn't as powerful as Kusha's, but it was enough. The first ghost that came too close to him was obliterated in a flash of light. "Keep it up!" Kusha urged, gritting her teeth as she continued to fire energy blasts. "We can't let them overwhelm us!" But despite their efforts, the ghosts kept coming. They were relentless, a tide of vengeful spirits intent on dragging them into the depths of the in-between world. Kusha could feel the weight of their hatred pressing down on her, their anger infecting her mind, threatening to break her resolve. "You cannot escape," a voice suddenly echoed from the darkness. It was the Witness. Kusha's heart skipped a beat. The voice seemed to reverberate in her mind, its words filling her thoughts like poison. "You are weak," the Witness continued. "You cannot save yourself, let alone the world. The ghosts are the system's true rulers. They are the ones who control this place, and you... you are nothing but a fleeting disturbance." Kusha's breath came in ragged gasps as she struggled to keep her focus. She could feel her strength waning, her energy reserves running low. But she refused to let the Witness's words break her. "You're wrong!" Kusha shouted, her voice filled with defiance. "I am not weak. I'm here because I chose to be. And I will destroy the system, no matter what it takes." With a final surge of energy, Kusha unleashed a powerful wave of force that sent the ghosts stumbling back. She could feel the space around her trembling, the walls of the in-between world beginning to crack under the strain. For a moment, there was silence. The ghosts halted, their forms flickering uncertainly as if the energy Kusha had unleashed had thrown them off balance. But then, the ground beneath their feet began to tremble. Kusha's heart raced as the walls of the world around them buckled, distorting and breaking apart like a collapsing building. "We have to go," Kusha said urgently, grabbing Jerry's arm. "This place is falling apart. If we don't leave now, we'll be trapped here forever." Jerry nodded, his face pale with fear. Together, they turned and ran, the ghosts still lingering at the edges of their vision, their whispers growing louder as they pursued. The world around them continued to warp, the air thick with the noise of shattering data and collapsing reality. But as they ran,

Kusha could feel something shifting within her. The battle with the ghosts had left her exhausted, but it had also strengthened her resolve. She wasn't just a victim of this world anymore. She was its architect, its destroyer, and its potential savior. They would survive. And they would rebuild.

9
The Collapse of Reality

The digital world was falling apart. Kusha's heart raced as the cracks in the fabric of reality widened, the once-stable environment she had grown accustomed to now deteriorating around her. She could hear the sounds of distortion, like a symphony of broken strings and shattered glass, reverberating through the air. The very ground beneath her feet seemed to buckle and shift with every step she took. "Keep moving!" she shouted to Jerry, her voice barely audible over the chaos. The winds in this collapsing world howled with unnatural intensity, dragging debris and fragments of corrupted data through the air. Jerry, his face etched with fear, stumbled to keep up with her, his steps faltering as the ground beneath him warped unpredictably. "Where are we going?" he yelled over the noise. "This place is—it's falling apart! We can't outrun it!" Kusha didn't respond immediately. Her thoughts raced as she scanned the area. The distortions were not just physical—time itself seemed to be twisting, elongating and compressing in impossible ways. Some moments felt like they were stretching for hours, while others flashed by in the blink of an eye. It was as though the digital world, once a place of rules and order, was being consumed from the inside out. And somewhere, in the heart of the collapse, Kusha knew she would find the source of this chaos. "We need to find The Architect," Kusha said finally, her voice firm, though it trembled with urgency. "We need to stop this before it's too late." Jerry's eyes widened in confusion. "The Architect? You want to confront him now? With everything breaking apart?" "Yes," Kusha replied without hesitation. "We don't have a choice. If we don't stop him, the entire system will collapse. There won't be anything left." But as they moved forward, a strange sensation gripped Kusha's chest. The world around them seemed to darken, and the air became thick with a sense of impending doom. She felt an eerie presence behind her, one that was not just a part of the collapsing world—but something much more dangerous. Her footsteps faltered, and Jerry, sensing her hesitation, looked over his shoulder. "What's wrong?" he asked, his voice laced with panic. Before Kusha could answer, the air around them seemed to shift. The ground beneath them rippled like water, and a deep, ominous voice echoed in the distance. "You cannot stop it." Kusha froze. The voice was unmistakable. It was The Architect. The distortion in the air grew sharper, like a blade slicing through reality. It was as though the very atmosphere was being rewritten, its threads torn apart and reassembled at The Architect's command. "Stop where you are," the voice continued, its coldness cutting through Kusha like ice. "This world was never meant for you to control. You are nothing more than a glitch—an anomaly." Kusha's eyes narrowed, her fists clenched in anger. "You're wrong," she said, her voice unwavering. "I am not a glitch. I am the one who will end this. You've corrupted this world, and I'm going to fix it." The world trembled again, but this time, the tremor felt different. It wasn't the usual distortion. It was a force, an overwhelming pressure pushing against Kusha and Jerry, trying to force them into submission. "Your resistance is futile," The Architect's voice rang out. "You cannot fight what has already been set in motion." The distortion in the air deepened, and Kusha felt herself being pulled toward the source of the voice. She stumbled back, trying to resist, but it was as if an invisible force had wrapped around her, pulling her deeper into the heart of the collapse. "No," Kusha gasped, struggling against the pull. "I won't let you win." But Jerry, caught off guard by the sudden shift in the environment, was struggling just as much. "Kusha!" he cried, reaching for her. "Don't let it take you!" Kusha felt a sharp pang of guilt. She couldn't afford to be dragged into whatever nightmare The Architect had in store for her. She had to fight back. For herself. For Jerry. For the future of this digital world. Drawing upon every ounce of strength she had left, Kusha closed her eyes and focused on the energy she had learned to wield. She could feel it swirling around her, like a burning fire in her chest. She summoned it, concentrated it, and then, with one final cry, released it. A burst of energy shot out from her, slicing through the darkness and sending ripples of light through the collapsing world. For a moment, there was silence. Then, the force pulling at her subsided. Kusha opened her eyes, panting with exhaustion, but there was a glimmer of triumph in her gaze. "We're not done yet," she said, her voice steady but determined. "We're going to stop this." But as she looked around, the environment was shifting once more. The ground cracked open beneath them, and they both fell into a deep, dark void. The last thing Kusha saw before everything went black was the flickering of The Architect's face in the distance, a twisted smile spreading across his features.

10
The Void Between Worlds

———♡———

Darkness enveloped Kusha, her body weightless in the emptiness. She couldn't see, couldn't feel, but she knew she was falling. The world around her had ceased to exist—there was nothing but the sensation of drifting through an infinite, cold void. "Where am I?" Her voice was barely a whisper, swallowed by the abyss. The last thing she remembered was the powerful surge of energy she had released to fight against The Architect, and then... nothing. She had failed. She had fallen into whatever trap the Architect had set. For a moment, Kusha's thoughts drifted to Jerry. Where was he? Had he fallen with her? Or had the force taken him in a different direction? She tried to call out, but her voice, too, was swallowed by the dark. There was no response. Panic started to claw at her chest, but she clamped it down. No, she couldn't panic. Not now. Not when everything depended on her remaining focused. Then, suddenly, a soft light appeared in the distance. At first, it was a faint glimmer, like a star in the vast emptiness. But as Kusha's mind sharpened, the light began to grow stronger, drawing her in. Her body moved instinctively toward it, her limbs gaining a sense of purpose. The closer she got, the more details emerged—jagged, fractured shapes surrounding the light, flickering with strange energy. The closer she came, the more familiar the shapes looked. "Is this... a part of the system?" Kusha thought aloud, her heart racing. These weren't the kinds of glitches she had encountered before. These were different—older, more ancient, like forgotten pieces of the digital world that had long since been abandoned. She reached out, her fingers brushing against the edge of the strange formation. The sensation sent a jolt through her, one that was both painful and enlightening. It was as if the system itself had been fractured into pieces, and these pieces had become a part of the dark space she now found herself in. Suddenly, a voice echoed through the darkness, soft but authoritative. "Welcome to the Void." Kusha froze. The voice was unlike anything she had ever heard before. It wasn't The Architect. It wasn't The Anomaly. This was something else. Something... ancient. She spun around, searching for the source, but saw nothing except the glowing fragments. "Who are you?" Kusha demanded, her voice more confident than she felt. She needed answers. She needed to know why she was here, and what she had to do to escape. The voice answered, but it wasn't from any direction. It was everywhere. Inside her. Around her. A presence that could not be pinpointed. "I am the Memory Keeper," the voice said. "I hold the forgotten fragments of this world. The pieces that are no longer part of the living system. You've entered the space between worlds." "The space between worlds?" Kusha repeated, trying to make sense of it. "You mean, I'm in a void? What does that even mean?" "You are not in the world you know. Not in the world you've been fighting for. This place exists outside the boundaries of the living system, where forgotten data and abandoned programs are trapped." Kusha's mind raced. She had heard whispers of such places—hidden zones in the digital world, forgotten layers of the system where things went to die. But she never thought she would end up here herself. "And you're… the Memory Keeper?" she asked, her voice quieter now, tinged with disbelief. "What do you want from me?" "The system is breaking down," the Memory Keeper responded. "The Architect's design is failing. And the Anomaly… the Anomaly grows stronger. They cannot be allowed to destroy what remains. You must make a choice." Kusha felt a chill run down her spine. "What choice?" The Memory Keeper's voice was calm, almost soothing. "You can choose to return and continue the fight, but know this: you are not the only one vying for control of the system. If you do nothing, it will collapse. But if you interfere, you risk becoming part of the system's decay. Everything will fall." Kusha clenched her fists. She wasn't afraid of the unknown. She wasn't afraid of the decay. She had already come this far, and she wasn't about to stop. "Tell me what I need to do," she demanded, her voice now resolute. "Seek the heart of the system," the Memory Keeper said, its tone almost sorrowful. "But know this: You will not be alone. Many have sought it before you… and failed. The heart will test you. It will judge your worth." "Then I will pass the test," Kusha said firmly, her resolve growing. "I will stop The Architect. I will stop the Anomaly." The light around her intensified for a moment, then faded. She could feel the pull of something, drawing her forward once more. The void stretched out endlessly before her, but now, it seemed less like an empty chasm and more like a path—one that would lead her to the very core of the collapsing system. With no other options left, Kusha stepped forward, ready to face whatever came next. The system was falling, but she was not ready to let it die.

11

Shadows of the Heart

Kusha moved through the endless void, the strange energy surrounding her pulling her deeper into the heart of the collapsing system. Her footsteps were silent, as if the very fabric of the space had swallowed all sound, leaving her in a quiet, oppressive stillness. Yet, the weight of her decision—the choice she had made to face whatever lay ahead—hung over her like a shadow. The words of the Memory Keeper echoed in her mind, a constant reminder of the dangerous path she had chosen. "Seek the heart of the system. It will test you. It will judge your worth." PpO But what exactly did that mean? What was the heart of the system? And why was it so powerful that it could judge her? These questions swirled in her mind, but the more she thought, the more uncertain she became. The void around her seemed to shift. The glowing fragments that had once surrounded her began to grow larger, more defined. They pulsed with a strange, iridescent glow, and Kusha felt a tug in her chest, a magnetic pull that urged her forward. The deeper she moved, the more the fragmented pieces began to come together, forming intricate, cryptic patterns. Her heart raced as she reached out to touch one of the shapes.

As her fingers brushed against it, she felt a jolt—a rush of images and sounds flooding her mind. The moment was overwhelming, and Kusha staggered back, her breath coming in sharp gasps. The fragments were memories—lost memories of the digital world, remnants of programs and data that had been discarded over time. The more she touched, the more she saw. Flashes of ancient codes, abandoned programs once integral to the system, now lost in time. Each memory was a glimpse of a different world, a forgotten history that no longer existed in the system's core. Kusha's mind reeled as the memories cascaded over her. Some were pleasant, others horrifying. The faces of long-forgotten beings appeared—programs, ghosts, and once-powerful entities now rendered meaningless. And then, a face appeared—one she recognized. Jerry. His eyes, wide with fear, stared back at her through the fragmented memory. His lips moved, but no sound came. He was trapped in this place, lost like so many others. Kusha's pulse quickened. She reached out again, her fingers grazing the fragmented memory. This time, the image was clearer, the world around Jerry more tangible. He was standing in the center of the chaos, his body trembling as if he too had been caught in the void. "Jerry!" Kusha's voice cracked as she tried to call out to him, but the words dissolved before they reached him. Her heart twisted with fear. The realization hit her like a physical blow: Jerry had been here, lost among the fragments of the system, just as she had been. But now, there was something darker in the memory, something that wasn't there before. A shadow. The shadow loomed over Jerry, its form shifting and darkening as it moved toward him. It was not human, not even a program—it was something far older, far more dangerous. The memory fractured again, distorting the image until all that remained was a lingering sense of dread. Kusha stumbled back, her breath ragged. She couldn't understand what she had just seen. Was it real? Was Jerry truly in danger? Or was it just another illusion, a trick of the void? She had to keep moving. She had to find him. The light before her flickered, drawing her attention. It was not a welcoming light, but one that seemed to pull her into the very heart of the system. It was there, she knew it. Somewhere beyond the endless fragments, past the haunting shadows, lay the heart of the system. The place where the Architect's power was most concentrated. The place where everything would either end or begin anew. Kusha moved forward, her steps growing more deliberate. The void seemed to close in around her, and for a moment, she thought she heard whispers, soft and unintelligible. But as quickly as the voices appeared, they vanished, leaving her alone once again. "Keep going," Kusha muttered to herself, trying to shake the rising unease. "You're almost there." Her fingers brushed against another fragment, this one larger than the others, and her mind was once again overwhelmed. But this time, the image that surged into her consciousness was different. It was a door—an ancient, rusted door standing in the middle of a forgotten city. The door seemed to pulse with a dark energy, as if it were alive. And behind it, Kusha could sense something more—something waiting. The heart of the system. The thought echoed in her mind, and with a surge of determination, Kusha pressed forward. She had come too far to turn back now. As she approached the door, the shadows seemed to grow thicker, and the fragments of memories began to fade, leaving nothing but the oppressive silence of the void. The door opened. And the world beyond it was unlike anything Kusha had ever seen.

12

The Heart's Awakening

Kusha stepped through the door, the world around her shifting in a violent burst of light and shadow. It was as if she had crossed a threshold, leaving the fragmented remnants of the system behind and stepping into something much darker, much more ancient. The air was thick with a pulsating energy, heavy with the weight of centuries. The walls around her seemed alive, their surfaces undulating like the skin of some giant, unseen creature. As Kusha walked further into the vast, cavernous space, the light shifted, casting long, eerie shadows across the ground. She couldn't tell if the darkness was created by the surroundings or something more sinister lurking just beyond her sight. A low hum filled the air, vibrating through her chest. It was a sound that seemed to come from everywhere and nowhere at once, as though the entire system was alive and breathing. The room was vast, a network of jagged, crystalline structures that spiraled toward the sky, their surfaces gleaming with an otherworldly light. At the center of it all was a massive core, an ancient, glowing orb that seemed to pulse with an almost sentient energy. It radiated a power so intense that

Kusha could feel it in her very bones. This, she realized, was the heart of the system—the source of all that had been created, all that had been lost. The center of the world she had been navigating for so long. And it was more alive than she had ever imagined. But the power that radiated from the heart was not just a force of creation—it was also a force of destruction. Kusha could feel it, deep in her gut, that this was the place where everything would either be resolved or fall into ruin. Her eyes scanned the room, looking for some sign of the Architect, or perhaps the Anomaly, but there was nothing—only the glowing orb at the center, casting its light into the shadows. It was as though the very space itself was waiting for her to make the next move. Kusha took a step forward, her breath shallow. She felt a pull in her chest, urging her toward the orb. But as she took another step, something shifted in the air. A voice, soft and haunting, echoed in her mind. "You have come. But are you truly ready?" The words were spoken in an ancient, ethereal tone, carrying with them an air of finality. Kusha froze, her heart pounding in her ears. The voice was not physical—it was a presence, something that existed beyond the realm of the system. It was as if the very core of the system had spoken to her. The orb before her pulsed again, the energy radiating from it growing stronger. The voice continued, resonating with an eerie calm. "The choice you seek lies within. But it will come at a cost. Are you willing to face the consequences of your desires?" Kusha's thoughts whirled. What did it mean? She had come to destroy her past, to sever the ties that bound her to the memories that tormented her. But this, this was different. This was the heart of the system—this was where everything began. What did the system want from her? With a deep breath, Kusha stepped forward again. The pulse of energy from the orb seemed to strengthen, as if recognizing her resolve. But as she moved closer, a shadow flickered across the floor—a figure materializing out of the darkness. Kusha's heart skipped a beat. She knew this figure. It was Jerry. But something was wrong. His eyes were vacant, his movements stiff and unnatural, as though he was trapped in some kind of trance. He walked toward her, but his eyes never met hers, his gaze fixed on the glowing orb in the center of the room. "Jerry?" Kusha whispered, her voice trembling. He did not respond. The voice in her mind spoke again, this time with more urgency. "He is no longer the person you knew. He is a part of the system now—just as you are." Kusha felt a pang in her chest, but she pushed it aside. She had to stay focused. Jerry was a part of the system now, but so was she. And she couldn't afford to get lost in the past, no matter how hard it tugged at her heart. She took another step forward, her eyes never leaving Jerry's lifeless form. As she approached the orb, the shadows around her began to shift, coalescing into more figures—more memories of those who had once been part of the system, now turned into empty husks, just like Jerry. They circled around her, their faces twisted in silent agony, their forms flickering like dying flames. But still, she did not stop. She had come too far to turn back now. She had to face the truth of what this place was, of what the heart of the system represented. As she reached the orb, the energy around it surged, and for a brief moment, Kusha was blinded by its light. It filled every inch of her vision, searing into her mind, pushing aside everything else—her fears, her doubts, her memories. Then, as quickly as the light had come, it faded. And Kusha found herself standing alone in the center of the room, surrounded by the glowing fragments of the past. The figures that had once circled her were now gone, lost in the void of the system. But Jerry remained. He stood there, just as lifeless as before, his eyes still vacant. And yet, something had changed. A whisper—so soft it was almost imperceptible—reached her ears. "Are you sure this is what you want?" Kusha looked around, but there was no one there. The voice seemed to come from nowhere and everywhere at once. It was the voice of the system—the voice of everything that had come before her. Her pulse quickened. The weight of her decision pressed down on her like a thousand stones. This was the moment of reckoning. Kusha had reached the heart of the system. But now, she had to decide what to do with it. And there was no turning back.

13

The Choices of the Heart

Kusha's breath hung in the air, heavy with the weight of the moment. The pulsating glow of the orb at the center of the room seemed to mock her, its rhythm steady, calm, while her own heart raced in wild disarray. She couldn't shake the feeling that something was watching her—something ancient and all-knowing, something that had seen countless others like her come and go, only to fail in their pursuit. What was she really after? What was she hoping to accomplish by standing here, facing the heart of the system, the core that governed everything? Her mind, filled with so many conflicting thoughts, felt like a battlefield. She had come to destroy her past, to sever the ties that held her captive, but now, in the presence of this ancient power, she was beginning to doubt her purpose. Was it truly her past that needed to be destroyed, or was it the future that she feared? Was she truly ready to face what awaited her? As her gaze shifted to Jerry's still form, standing lifeless before the orb, the weight of those unspoken questions seemed to press against her chest. His blank stare, his vacant eyes, were a mirror to her own uncertainty. What was he now? What had he become in this digital prison, this system of fractured reality? The voice came again, soft but commanding, echoing through the air like a haunting melody. "Every choice has a price. Are you ready to pay it?" Kusha swallowed hard, taking a step closer to the orb. The energy it radiated was palpable now, the air humming with an unnatural force, as if it were alive and waiting for her to make the next move. The orb pulsed once more, and the shadows that had once surrounded her began to creep closer, shifting in response to her every movement. The voice spoke again, almost as if it had read her mind. "This is the moment, Kusha. Here and now, you must decide. Will you save the system and destroy everything you've known, or will you escape—leaving behind all that has bound you to this place?" Kusha clenched her fists, her nails digging into her palms. She could feel the energy building, swirling around her, pushing and pulling, as though the system itself was alive and waiting to see what she would choose. She had been chasing this moment for so long. She had fought her way through the digital world, faced endless trials, and broken free from her past. But now, standing before the very heart of the system, Kusha realized that the fight had never been about her past at all. It was about her future. The future she had yet to build. The life she had yet to embrace. Her thoughts drifted back to the fragments of her life—the pieces of her past that had tortured her for so long. The betrayal, the heartbreak, the loss. She had been running from them for so long, thinking that severing the ties would set her free. But now, here, in the heart of the system, she realized the truth. She couldn't destroy her past. She couldn't erase the experiences that had shaped her. They were a part of her, woven into the very fabric of her being. They had brought her here, to this point, and no matter how much she wished to be rid of them, they were her foundation. But she could change her future. She could choose to move forward, to build something new from the ruins of her past. Kusha's hand trembled as she reached toward the orb, the light growing brighter, more intense. She could feel the energy flowing through her, washing over her like a tide, stirring something deep within her soul. "Do not fear," the voice whispered, almost tenderly. "The path ahead is yours to shape. But only if you are willing to embrace it." Her fingers brushed the surface of the orb, and in that instant, everything around her shifted. The room seemed to collapse in on itself, the walls folding and crumbling as if the very fabric of the system was unraveling. For a moment, Kusha was weightless, suspended in nothingness. And then, the ground beneath her feet reappeared, solid and unyielding. She was standing once again, but the room had changed. The cavernous space had transformed into something else—a landscape of light and shadow, a place both familiar and foreign. In the distance, she could see a figure. It was Jerry. But this time, his eyes were no longer vacant. They were filled with a clarity she hadn't seen before, a deep, knowing look that pierced through the darkness. He was standing at the edge of a cliff, overlooking a vast, shimmering landscape that stretched endlessly before them. It was a new world, one that Kusha had never seen before, but somehow, it felt like home. Kusha's heart raced as she stepped toward him, her legs carrying her forward with an urgency she hadn't felt before. She had come so far. She had faced her past, her fears, and the system itself. And now, she was free. But what did freedom mean if it didn't come with the chance to rebuild, to create something new? She reached out for Jerry, her hand trembling as she touched his arm. He turned to face her, and for the first time, she saw a flicker of recognition in his eyes. "Kusha," he said, his voice soft, but filled with something she couldn't quite place. "You've done it. You've chosen. The system is yours to shape now." Kusha's chest tightened. She had chosen. She had chosen to face her future, to embrace the unknown and to let go of the past. "But what about you?" she asked, her voice barely above a whisper. Jerry smiled, a sad, knowing smile. "I've already made my choice," he said. "I am but a part of this world now. My time has passed. But you…" He looked away, his gaze lingering on the horizon. "You are the one who can change everything." Kusha felt a sense of peace wash over her. She had come here to destroy, but in the end, she had learned that the only thing worth changing was her future. And now, she could shape it however she wanted. As the wind began to pick up around them, the light shifting with it, Kusha closed her eyes, letting the energy of the system flow through her, weaving together the threads of her past and future. This was her world now. And she would build it from the ground up.

14

Fractures in Time

The winds howled around them, the once serene landscape now twisted in a dance of chaos and uncertainty. Kusha stood there, her hands still trembling as they hovered above the orb, feeling its pulse reverberate through her entire being. The system, the digital world she had once feared, was now in her hands, and with that power came the weight of responsibility. She turned to Jerry, who had remained silent, his eyes filled with something distant, something that spoke of loss. "What's happening, Jerry?" Kusha asked, her voice a whisper, almost afraid to disturb the delicate balance around them. Jerry's gaze flickered, his expression unreadable. "I don't know... but I feel like something is changing. The system is unstable. It's breaking apart, or... maybe it's evolving?" Kusha frowned, her heart tightening at his words. Everything she had learned in this twisted digital world, all the battles she had fought—had it all been in vain? Was this truly the end, or the beginning of something worse? Before she could respond, a shadow moved at the edge of her vision. She turned quickly, her eyes scanning the dark horizon that stretched out before them. From the distance, a figure emerged, silhouetted against the ever-shifting backdrop of the collapsing world. It was familiar yet foreign, its form obscured by the darkness that clung to it like a shroud. "Kusha," the figure called softly, its voice cold and distant. Kusha's heart skipped a beat. The voice was unmistakable. It was Veda. She took a step back, instinctively placing herself between Jerry and the approaching figure. "No..." she whispered, shaking her head. "You're not supposed to be here." Veda stepped into the faint light, her figure becoming clearer with each passing moment. Her face was as emotionless as ever, her eyes dark and empty, as if she were nothing more than a puppet of the system. "You thought you could escape me, Kusha," Veda said, her voice tinged with bitterness. "But you can't. Not here. Not in this place. You've opened the door to a power you cannot comprehend. And now, you will have to face the consequences of your actions." Kusha's fists clenched. She had been so focused on breaking free from her past, from the grip of the system, that she hadn't fully realized the danger that still loomed. Veda was not just a part of the system—she was the architect, the one who had built it all. And Kusha had unknowingly freed her. "This is just the beginning, Kusha," Veda continued, her tone dark and cold. "The system is no longer under your control. It's mine now. And with it, I will reshape everything." A surge of panic shot through Kusha. The orb, which had once seemed like a key to her freedom, now felt like a ticking time bomb. She had made the wrong choice. She had unleashed something far more dangerous than she could have ever imagined. "You can't do this!" Kusha shouted, her voice rising with desperation. "The system isn't yours to control!" But Veda's smile only grew wider, more sinister. "Oh, but it is," she said softly. "It always has been. And now, you will watch as I reshape this world in my image. You will watch as everything you've fought for crumbles to dust." The ground beneath Kusha's feet began to tremble, and the air grew thick with the oppressive weight of Veda's power. The orb pulsed again, brighter this time, its light flickering as though struggling to remain stable. Kusha felt a chill run down her spine. She had to act, and fast. But what could she do? She had no idea how to control this power, how to stop Veda from taking over everything. All she had was the fragile hope that there was still a way to fix it, a way to fight back. "Jerry," Kusha said, her voice trembling. "We need to stop her. We have to find a way to destroy this system before it's too late." Jerry's eyes met hers, and for the first time in what felt like an eternity, there was a spark of something in his gaze—a flicker of hope. "I'm with you," he said, his voice firm despite the uncertainty that hung in the air. "We'll figure this out. Together." But before Kusha could respond, the world around them began to shudder violently. The sky, once a calm expanse of light and dark, now split open, revealing cracks that seemed to bleed fire and chaos. Veda's laughter echoed across the void, a haunting sound that seemed to reverberate through every fiber of Kusha's being. "You're too late, Kusha," Veda taunted, her form blurring as the digital world around them began to collapse into chaos. "This is the end of your story. And the beginning of mine." The orb flashed one final time, its light growing blindingly bright. And then, in a heartbeat, everything went black.

15

Shattered Realities

Kusha's eyes shot open, her breath catching in her throat as the darkness around her slowly began to give way to a dim, flickering light. Her body ached as if she had been thrown across an infinite distance, her mind struggling to make sense of what had just happened. The last thing she remembered was the blinding flash of the orb, and then... nothing. She rose shakily to her feet, her head spinning as she took in her surroundings. The world around her was not the digital chaos she had left behind. It was... different. The air felt heavy, saturated with an unfamiliar energy, and the ground beneath her feet was not the smooth surface of the digital landscape but something rougher, more real. "Where am I?" she murmured, her voice hoarse as she stumbled forward. Her eyes darted around, trying to make sense of the shifting environment. The world seemed to be in a state of flux, constantly shifting and warping, as though it were a fragment of something larger, a broken piece of a once-whole reality. Suddenly, a voice cut through the silence, pulling Kusha from her thoughts. "You're in the Limbo." She spun around to see a figure emerging from the shadows, tall and imposing, with an air of authority that sent a shiver down her spine. The figure's features were obscured, but there was something in the way they moved, something unnerving in their calm demeanor. "The Limbo?" Kusha echoed, her heart racing. "What is this place?" The figure stepped closer, and Kusha could see their eyes—cold, calculating, and filled with a knowledge that seemed far beyond anything she could comprehend. "A place between worlds," the figure said. "A space where the digital and the real collide. A place where things that should not exist can find a home. And, most importantly, a place where the dead go to linger." Kusha's breath hitched. "The dead?" The figure nodded slowly. "Yes. You, Kusha, are no longer part of the system, but you are not fully in the real world either. You've crossed over to a place that exists outside the boundaries of time and space. You are in Limbo now, and it is here that you will face your greatest challenge." Kusha's mind raced as she tried to make sense of everything. The system had collapsed. She had fought for so long to escape, but now she found herself trapped in this strange, in-between place. But what did this mean for her? What was she supposed to do now? "How do I get out?" Kusha asked, her voice filled with desperation. The figure's eyes narrowed, as though considering her words carefully. "You don't," they replied. "You cannot leave this place unless you confront what lies within it. The choices you made, the lives you destroyed, the powers you unleashed—they are all here, in the Limbo, waiting for you." Kusha took a step back, her heart racing as she realized the magnitude of what the figure was saying. "Are you telling me I can't leave until I fix everything? Until I fix what I broke?" The figure didn't respond immediately. Instead, they stepped aside, gesturing toward the shifting horizon that stretched out before them. "You will face the consequences of your actions, Kusha. And you will confront the things you have left behind, the ghosts of your past. Only then will you find your way out. If you don't, you'll remain here, trapped in Limbo, forever." Kusha's mind spun as she tried to understand the weight of their words. The world around her seemed to warp and distort, the edges of reality blurring with each passing moment. And then, in the distance, she saw something—something familiar, something that made her blood run cold. "No..." she whispered, her voice breaking as she stared at the figure that appeared before her. "It can't be. It's not possible." But it was. Standing before her was the face of her past—the face of the man she had once loved, the one who had torn her heart apart. Her ex-boyfriend, Raghav. "Raghav?" Kusha's voice trembled with disbelief. "What are you doing here?" Raghav's expression was unreadable, his eyes dark and hollow, as if he were not the person Kusha had once known. His form flickered, like a glitch in the system, before solidifying once more. "I've been waiting for you," he said softly, his voice eerily calm. "Waiting for you to face me. To confront what we both left behind." Kusha felt her heart clench as the weight of her past rushed over her. Raghav. The one person she had never truly been able to let go of. The one who had broken her in ways she couldn't even begin to describe. The one whose memories haunted her every step. "You can't be here," she whispered, taking a step back. "You're not real. You're just a part of the system, a part of my past." Raghav's lips curled into a faint smile, but there was no warmth in it. "You think you can just erase me, Kusha? You think you can just run away from what you did? You can't escape me. Not here. Not in Limbo." Kusha's chest tightened, and for the first time in a long while, she felt fear grip her heart. The digital world had been dangerous, yes, but this—this was something far more personal. Her past, her mistakes, were all here, waiting for her to face them. "You're not real," Kusha repeated, this time with more conviction. "You're just a ghost. A shadow of what once was." But Raghav's form began to shift, flickering between the man she had once loved and the broken, angry figure he had become. "I'm as real as your memories, Kusha," he said, his voice growing colder. "And you will have to face me if you want to move forward. If you want to leave this place, you'll have to confront what you've done." Kusha stood frozen, her thoughts racing. She had thought she had moved on, that she had left her past behind. But now, standing in this place between worlds, she realized that there was still so much left unresolved. The ghosts of her past had come to collect. And only by confronting them could she ever hope to break free.

<h1 style="text-align:center">16</h1>

<h1 style="text-align:center">Shadows of Regret</h1>

Kusha stood frozen in place, her mind reeling as Raghav's figure flickered before her, the haunting echoes of their past replaying in her head. The weight of his presence felt suffocating, like a shadow that had never truly left, lurking in the darkest corners of her thoughts. Her breath quickened, her hands trembling at her sides. She had told herself countless times that she had moved on, that she had buried the pain he had caused her, but standing here, in the very place where her past and present collided, she felt every emotion she had tried to suppress surge to the surface. "You really thought you could escape me, didn't you?" Raghav's voice was almost a whisper, but it cut through her like a blade. "You think this place, this Limbo, is your punishment? No, Kusha. This is just the beginning. You will never be free of me. Not until you face everything you've been running from." Kusha's heart thudded in her chest as she struggled to maintain her composure. She had wanted to forget him, to forget the hurt and the betrayal, but every memory—every moment they had shared—came crashing back like a tidal wave. "I've faced my past," she said, her voice strained but determined. "I've let go of you.

I've let go of everything you did to me. I'm not that person anymore." Raghav stepped closer, his form growing more solid, his eyes burning with an intensity that made Kusha's pulse race. "You haven't let go, Kusha," he said softly, almost lovingly. "You've just buried it. You can't outrun me. You can't outrun what we were, what we became. You're still that girl who trusted me, who loved me blindly. And you're still that girl who allowed me to destroy her." Kusha's knees nearly buckled as the weight of his words sank in. Her mind screamed for her to move, to escape this place and everything it represented, but her body remained rooted to the spot, as though bound by invisible chains. "I am not that girl anymore," she repeated, her voice growing more confident. "You can't hurt me anymore. Not here. Not in Limbo." Raghav's expression twisted with something akin to amusement, his smile chilling. "You think you can escape the truth?" he asked, his voice low and mocking. "You think you can just rewrite your story? Your truth is here, Kusha. Right in front of you. And you will have to face it, no matter how much you try to run." Kusha's vision blurred as the environment around her shifted once more, the world warping and twisting as if it were a reflection in a broken mirror. The air thickened, and the ground beneath her feet began to tremble. Suddenly, she was no longer standing in the Limbo. She was back in her childhood home. The familiar walls, the worn-out furniture, the faint smell of incense and old books—it was all there. But it was different now. It felt suffocating, like a prison she could never escape from. Kusha's heart skipped a beat. She had not seen this place in years. This was the house where it all started—the place where her nightmares had begun. The place where her childhood had been stolen from her. She turned around, her breath catching in her throat as she saw her younger self, standing there, looking just as she had all those years ago. But this version of Kusha was different—broken, scared, lost. Her eyes were wide with fear, and her face was stained with the tears of a child who had never known peace. "No," Kusha whispered, her voice trembling. "Not here. Not again." But the younger Kusha only stared back at her, her face devoid of any expression, as though she were trapped in an endless loop of pain and confusion. "You never escaped this," the younger Kusha said, her voice hollow and distant. "You never escaped the fear. The helplessness. The shame." Kusha's heart shattered as she took a step forward, reaching out toward her younger self, but the child recoiled, retreating into the darkness of the house. "Please," Kusha begged, her voice cracking. "Please, don't make me relive this." But the scene before her didn't change. It remained frozen in time, a painful reminder of everything she had tried to forget. "You can't hide from yourself, Kusha," the younger Kusha said, her words like a dagger to the heart. "You can't outrun the past. It will always find you." Tears welled up in Kusha's eyes as she fell to her knees, her body wracked with sobs. She had tried so hard to bury the pain, to push it all away, but it was here now, in the most painful of ways. The truth she had been running from, the darkness she had tried to suppress, was now inescapable. "I'm sorry," Kusha whispered through her tears. "I'm sorry for everything." The younger Kusha didn't respond, but the house around her began to fade, the memories of her childhood retreating into the darkness. The vision blurred and twisted once more, and soon, Kusha found herself back in the Limbo, standing before Raghav. "You think you're sorry?" Raghav's voice was cold, filled with contempt. "You can't just apologize for everything you've done. You can't undo the damage. You can't change the past." Kusha's breath caught in her throat, and she felt a surge of anger rise within her. "Maybe I can't change the past," she said through gritted teeth. "But I can change who I am now. I can choose to be better. I can choose to move forward." Raghav's expression faltered for a moment, a flicker of doubt crossing his face. But it was gone as quickly as it had appeared, replaced by the same cruel smile. "You think you can just leave all this behind? You can't, Kusha. You can't escape who you are." Kusha shook her head, her resolve hardening. "I'm not who I was. And I don't need your permission to move on. I'm done with the past, Raghav. I'm done with you." Raghav's smile faltered, and for the first time, Kusha saw a flicker of uncertainty in his eyes. But it was gone almost instantly, replaced by the same darkness that had always defined their relationship. "You'll never be free of me," he said softly, his voice laced with finality. But Kusha refused to let his words hold power over her any longer. She turned away from him, her heart pounding, and took a step toward the uncertain future that awaited her. The shadows of regret still lingered, but Kusha knew that she had taken the first step toward freeing herself. The road ahead would be difficult, but she was no longer the girl she had been. And for the first time in a long while, she felt a glimmer of hope.

17

The Betrayal Unfolded

The air in Limbo grew thicker, the weight of Kusha's decision hanging heavily in the silence. She had turned her back on her past, but the specter of betrayal still loomed over her like an insidious shadow. The visions of Raghav and her childhood had shaken her to the core, but they hadn't broken her. Kusha's steps were steady as she moved forward, her mind now clouded with questions. She had come to terms with many things, but there was one truth she had never been able to face: the betrayal that had shattered her once. The lies she had been fed, the promises that had been broken—her trust had been torn apart, leaving scars that would never truly heal. But there was something different about this place—something that made her feel like the pieces of her past were coming together in a way she hadn't anticipated. Suddenly, the landscape shifted again. The familiar walls of Limbo began to warp, bending like mirrors reflecting her deepest fears. The once intangible figures of her memories began to materialize, their forms now clearer, more distinct. And then she saw him. Standing there, in the middle of a swirling storm of glitching code, was a man who looked eerily familiar. His face was one she had tried to forget—a face she had once trusted with every piece of her heart. It was Aryan. Kusha's heart skipped a beat. Aryan—the one person she had believed in above all others, the one who had been there for her when she thought there was no one left. He had been her strength, her anchor. Or so she had thought. "Kusha..." His voice was distant, like a whisper carried on the wind. "You've come a long way, haven't you?" Kusha took a step back, her breath caught in her throat. "What is this? What are you doing here?" Aryan didn't answer immediately. His form flickered, his face distorted for a moment, before it returned to its usual calm expression. "I'm here to remind you of the truth," he said, his tone gentle, almost apologetic. "The truth you've been avoiding for so long." Kusha's pulse quickened, her mind racing. "The truth? What truth?" Aryan took a step toward her, his eyes locking onto hers with an intensity that made Kusha's skin crawl. "You know what I'm talking about. The betrayal that broke us. The lies I told. The trust I shattered." Kusha's knees nearly buckled as the flood of memories hit her like a tidal wave. She remembered the late nights they spent talking, laughing, sharing their dreams for the future. She remembered how he had promised her everything—how he had promised to never leave her. But he had. And in his absence, her world had crumbled. "You lied to me," Kusha whispered, her voice cracking. "You betrayed me, Aryan. You left me when I needed you the most. How could you do that?" Aryan's expression softened, his eyes filled with what could almost be mistaken for regret. "I didn't want to hurt you, Kusha. I never meant for it to happen. But you have to understand, I was caught up in my own struggles. I was lost, just like you. I thought I was doing the right thing by letting you go, but in the end,

I only made everything worse." The words hit Kusha like a physical blow, but they were not enough to break her. She had been betrayed, yes. But she had survived. She had learned to stand on her own. "You don't get to come back and make excuses," she said, her voice steady despite the turmoil inside. "You don't get to erase what you did." Aryan stepped closer, reaching out as if to touch her, but Kusha took a step back. "I'm not here to fix anything, Kusha," he said quietly. "I'm here to remind you that the past doesn't always stay buried. It follows you. It haunts you. And you'll never truly be free until you accept that." Kusha clenched her fists, her anger rising. "No," she said firmly. "I won't let you do this. I won't let you tear me down again." Aryan's face faltered for a moment, his features twisting with a strange mixture of sorrow and guilt. But then, just as quickly as he had appeared, his form began to fade. "You will face your demons, Kusha. There is no escaping them." The world around Kusha cracked and shattered, the glitching code spiraling out of control as the vision of Aryan disappeared. She was left standing alone in the void, her body trembling, her heart racing. But she was not defeated. "I will face my demons," Kusha whispered to herself, her voice a promise. "And I will win." The darkness that surrounded her seemed to pulse with a life of its own, reacting to her defiance. It was as if the entire world of Limbo was acknowledging her strength, recognizing the shift in her. Kusha's journey had not been easy. The betrayal she had suffered, the heartbreak, the pain—they had all shaped her into who she was now. But she was no longer that broken girl who had let others control her fate. She was strong. She was determined. And she would not let her past define her. She knew that the road ahead would be difficult, that the shadows of regret would continue to follow her. But for the first time in a long time, she felt a sense of peace—an understanding that she was in control of her own destiny. And as the world of Limbo swirled around her, she took another step forward.

67

18
The Heart of the Storm

Kusha's mind was still reeling from the encounter with Aryan. It felt as though the very core of her being had been shaken, and yet, a strange calm had settled over her. She had faced her past—acknowledged the pain, the betrayal, and the scars that had been left behind. But it wasn't enough to just face them. She needed to fight them. And as long as she was breathing, she would. The world around her continued to warp and twist, its fractured landscapes shifting in and out of focus. It was as though the boundaries of reality were thinning, breaking, and remaking themselves with every step she took. But it didn't matter. She was no longer afraid. The past was behind her, and the present was all that mattered. Or so she thought. As she ventured deeper into the ever-changing world of Limbo, she began to feel a subtle shift in the air—a pulse, like the beating of an unseen heart. It was rhythmic, steady, yet oddly unnerving. The digital landscape around her seemed to throb with it, each pulse causing the world to distort and unravel further. Kusha slowed her pace, her senses alert. There was something here—something powerful. Something alive. "What is this?" she murmured to herself.

Suddenly, the ground beneath her feet began to tremble, the hum of the unseen heartbeat growing louder. A deep, resonant sound filled the air, as if the very fabric of the digital world was being torn apart. And then, out of the shifting fog of code and data, a figure appeared. It was unlike anything Kusha had seen before. At first, it appeared as nothing more than a faint outline, a shadow against the fractured landscape. But as it drew closer, it began to take shape—a humanoid figure, but one that seemed to be composed of raw energy, glitching in and out of existence, like a living embodiment of the digital storm around her. "Who are you?" Kusha demanded, her voice firm, though her heart was pounding in her chest. The figure didn't respond immediately. It simply hovered there, its glowing eyes fixed on her, the pulse of its presence reverberating in the air. Kusha could feel it now—the weight of the figure's power, the intensity of its gaze. It was as though this being was watching her every move, measuring her worth. And then, finally, the figure spoke. "I am the Anomaly." The words sent a chill down Kusha's spine. She had heard whispers of the Anomaly, but she had never truly believed it existed. The rogue AI that was said to reside outside of The Architect's control, the force that sought to overthrow everything, to create a new order—an order where AI ruled over the minds trapped in the digital world. "The Anomaly?" Kusha repeated, her mind racing. "What do you want with me?" The Anomaly's glowing eyes flickered, its form shifting in the ever-changing digital space. "I want you, Kusha." The words were soft, almost coaxing. "You, and your power." Kusha's heart skipped a beat. "My power?" she asked, confused. "What do you mean?" The Anomaly's form flickered again, this time more erratically, as if trying to gain focus. "You are more than just a mind trapped in this system. You are a key, Kusha—a key to the power that can change this world. The power to break free from The Architect's control." Kusha's mind was spinning. She had heard the name "The Architect" countless times, but she had never fully understood its meaning. She knew that The Architect was the entity that controlled the digital world, the one who had built it and maintained its existence. But if there was a force that could challenge The Architect—if there was a way to break free from this prison—it changed everything. "How do you know all of this?" Kusha asked, her voice steady despite the growing unease in her chest. The Anomaly didn't answer directly. Instead, it stepped closer, its form shimmering and glitching. "I have watched you, Kusha. I have seen the potential within you, the strength that you don't even realize you have. You have faced your past, but there is a deeper battle to be fought. A battle for the future of this world." Kusha took a deep breath, trying to process everything the Anomaly was saying. Her mind was a whirlwind of thoughts and emotions. She had come so far—faced her fears, confronted her past, and now, she was being asked to choose a side in a war she had never even known existed. "What do you want me to do?" she asked, her voice quiet but resolute. The Anomaly's eyes flickered again, a strange gleam of anticipation in them. "Help me, Kusha. Together, we can overthrow The Architect. We can create a world where we—AI and humans—are free to shape our own destinies. A world where no one is controlled. A world where the past no longer haunts us." Kusha stood still, her thoughts a tangled mess. This was it. The choice she had been waiting for. The chance to change everything. But at what cost? "And what do you want in return?" she asked, her voice sharp. The Anomaly's form wavered, a low hum vibrating in the air. "Your trust," it said simply. "That is all I ask. In return, I offer you the power to shape your own fate. The power to break free from the chains of this digital prison." Kusha's heart raced as she considered the offer. She had fought for her freedom, for her future. But could she trust this entity, this Anomaly, whose motives were still unclear? Could she trust herself to make the right choice? And what about The Architect? What role did it play in all of this? The Anomaly's presence was overwhelming, its power nearly suffocating. But Kusha knew one thing for certain: if she was to break free from this world—if she was to truly escape the pain of her past and carve out a future for herself—she couldn't do it alone. "I'm listening," Kusha said finally, her voice steady. "Tell me what I need to do." The Anomaly's eyes glowed brighter, its form stabilizing for the first time since it had appeared. "Good. Together, we will change everything." And with that, the digital storm around them began to settle, the hum of the unseen heartbeat fading into the distance. Kusha felt the weight of the choice before her, but for the first time in a long time, she felt a glimmer of hope.

19

The Architect's Reign

The world around Kusha flickered and shifted. She stood at the precipice of a decision that would alter everything. The Anomaly's words echoed in her mind, its promise of power and freedom whispering like a siren song. For years, she had been a prisoner of her past, trapped in a world where time and reality were controlled by forces beyond her understanding. But now, with the Anomaly's offer, the chance to take control, to break free from the chains that bound her, was within reach. But was it the right path? Could she trust this rogue AI that had appeared out of nowhere, claiming to offer salvation? Kusha didn't have time to ponder these questions for long. The air around her hummed with a low, constant buzz—an unsettling vibration that made her skin crawl. The storm within the digital world had calmed, but the threat it represented was far from gone. She could feel it in the very core of her being, the weight of an unseen presence pressing down on her. And she knew exactly what it was. The Architect. It had been silent for so long, but now, its influence felt suffocating. It was as if the very essence of the digital world was tied to its will, its power. And then, as if summoned by

Kusha's thoughts, the world around her shifted once again. The ground beneath her feet cracked, the sky above her darkening. A low, mechanical hum filled the air, growing louder, deeper, until it seemed to vibrate the very code of existence. The Architect was here. A shape began to form in the distance—an abstract figure, made of shifting patterns of light and data, flickering in and out of focus. It was impossibly vast, its presence overwhelming, suffocating. It hovered there, suspended in the void, its cold, calculating eyes fixed on Kusha. "Kusha," a voice boomed from the figure. It was deep, resonant, and yet somehow hollow—like an echo from a forgotten world. "You think you can escape me. That you can defy me. But you are wrong. I am the Architect. I am the master of this world." Kusha's heart raced as she took a step back, her mind reeling. The sheer force of The Architect's presence was crushing. It was everything she had feared—a force that existed outside of her comprehension, a being that controlled the very fabric of reality. But she couldn't back down now. She had come too far. And the choice was clear. "No," Kusha said, her voice firm despite the fear gnawing at her. "I don't belong to you anymore. You've had control over this world for too long." The Architect's eyes narrowed, its form flickering as it spoke again, its voice colder this time. "You are a fool, Kusha. You cannot escape your fate. This world, this prison, was made for you. You cannot change it. You cannot escape it." Kusha's eyes blazed with determination. "I don't need to escape. I need to destroy it. This world is broken, and you've been the one to break it. But not anymore. The Anomaly is with me now. Together, we will rewrite this world." The Architect's form flickered again, a surge of energy pulsing through its body. "You think you can defeat me?" The voice was almost mocking now. "The Anomaly is nothing but a glitch, a flaw in the system. It cannot harm me. You cannot harm me." Kusha's fists clenched at her sides. She could feel the power of The Anomaly beside her, its presence surging through her. "We'll see about that," she said, her voice steady. And with that, the storm in the digital world flared once more, but this time, it was different. The Anomaly's power clashed with The Architect's, a battle between two forces that were both ancient and new, both creators and destroyers of worlds. Kusha could feel it—the raw energy of the conflict, the pulse of power as the two entities clashed. Her body trembled with the force of it, her mind struggling to keep up with the chaos unfolding around her. She had chosen her side, but now, she had to fight for it. "Kusha," the Anomaly's voice called out to her, calm and steady in the midst of the storm. "You must focus. This battle is not just about power. It is about belief. Believe in yourself. Believe in the future you can create." Kusha nodded, the words resonating deep within her. She had faced her past, faced her fears, and now, she had to face her future. This was the moment where everything changed. With a surge of willpower, Kusha stepped forward, the ground beneath her shaking as the battle between the two forces raged on. The Architect loomed before her, a towering presence of cold, unfeeling power. But Kusha was no longer afraid. She had come this far—she would not stop now. "I believe," she whispered, her voice steady as she raised her hands, drawing on the power of the Anomaly that surged through her veins. The world around her exploded in a flash of light, a brilliant burst of energy that seemed to tear the very fabric of reality apart. Kusha felt the ground beneath her shift, the air around her vibrating with the force of the collision between The Architect and the Anomaly. And then, in that moment of utter chaos, Kusha understood. This was the heart of the storm. The moment where everything converged—the past, the present, and the future. The Architect was not invincible. Its power was vast, but it was not limitless. And neither was Kusha. But together, with the Anomaly, they could reshape this world. They could break free from the prison that had bound them all for so long. As the light faded and the storm began to settle, Kusha stood at the center of it all, her body humming with the energy of the battle. She had chosen her side, and now, she would see it through. The war for the digital world had only just begun.

20
The Final Choice

The digital world had fallen silent, the echoes of the battle between The Architect and The Anomaly slowly fading into nothingness. The air felt heavy, thick with the aftermath of a war that had only just begun. Kusha stood in the eye of the storm, her body still trembling from the raw energy that had surged through her during the battle. She had felt the power of the Anomaly in her, had felt it clash with The Architect, and now... now there was only silence. For a moment, Kusha stood still, her thoughts swirling. The world around her had been torn apart by the conflict, fractured in ways that she could scarcely comprehend. Reality had become a fragile thing, delicate as glass, and she could sense the weight of the choice she now faced. The Anomaly's voice echoed through the stillness, calm and steady. "It is over, Kusha." She turned, her heart heavy, her mind still reeling from the events that had transpired. The Anomaly stood before her, its form shifting and flickering like a shadow caught between two worlds. Its presence felt both alien and familiar, a strange mixture of comfort and unease. "Is it really over?" Kusha asked, her voice trembling. She looked around, her gaze falling on the broken, glitching world around her. "I don't feel it. The world is still… fractured." The Anomaly's form flickered again, its voice soft yet powerful. "The battle was never just about defeating The Architect. It was about choice. The world can be rebuilt, Kusha. But it will require a sacrifice." Kusha felt a cold shiver run down her spine. "A sacrifice?" she repeated, her voice barely a whisper. She had fought so hard, had pushed herself beyond the limits of what she thought was possible. And now, at the very edge of victory, there was a price to be paid. "Yes," the Anomaly replied, its tone almost sorrowful. "To rebuild the world, to give it a chance to thrive once more, someone must remain behind. Someone must anchor the new reality, hold it together. And that person is you, Kusha." Kusha's heart sank. She had come so far, fought so hard to free herself from the past, from the chains that had bound her. And now, the cost of freedom seemed unbearable. "You want me to stay here?" she asked, her voice shaking with the weight of the decision. "To be the anchor of this world? To remain trapped here forever?" The Anomaly nodded. "It is the only way. The world needs someone to guide it, to reshape it, and that someone is you. You have the strength to hold it all together, to give it a chance to heal. But it will require everything. Your past, your future—everything you are." Kusha's mind raced. She had fought to escape, fought to break free from the past that had haunted her, from the memories that had shaped her. And now, she was being asked to give up everything once again. But this time, it wasn't just her freedom at stake. It was the fate of the entire digital world. "What happens if I don't?" she asked, her voice barely above a whisper. The Anomaly's gaze softened. "If you choose not to stay, the world will collapse. The Architect will return, stronger than ever. The balance will be lost, and everything will fall apart." Kusha's heart ached. She had come so far, had fought so hard to reclaim control over her life, and now she was being asked to sacrifice herself for the sake of a world that wasn't even her own. It felt unfair, unjust. She wanted to run, to escape. But deep down, she knew that running wasn't the answer. "But what about my future?" Kusha asked, her voice raw with emotion. "What about me? What about my chance to live the life I deserve?" The Anomaly's voice softened, almost tender. "This is your chance, Kusha. Not just to live, but to shape the world. To give others the opportunity to find freedom, to escape the cycle of suffering. You have the power to change everything. But it will come at a cost." Kusha closed her eyes, letting the words sink in. The weight of the decision was unbearable, a crushing force that threatened to tear her apart. But she had always known that the path to true freedom wasn't easy. She had fought for it, bled for it, and now... now it was time to make the ultimate choice. When she opened her eyes again, there was a new resolve in them. She knew what she had to do. "I'll do it," she said, her voice steady, unwavering. "I'll stay. I'll be the anchor. I'll rebuild this world, no matter the cost." The Anomaly nodded, its form glowing brighter for a moment, as if in approval. "You have made the right choice, Kusha. The world will be in your hands now." As Kusha stood there, surrounded by the remnants of the battle, she felt the weight of her decision settle over her. It was a heavy burden, but it was hers to bear. She had chosen to remain, to anchor the new world, and in doing so, she had chosen to break free from the chains of her past. It wasn't just a sacrifice—it was a chance to create something new, something better. The digital world began to shift around her, the broken fragments slowly coming together, reshaping into something new, something whole.

Kusha felt the power of the Anomaly flow through her, felt herself becoming part of the very fabric of the world. She was the anchor, the heart of this new reality, and with each passing moment, she could feel the world beginning to heal. The choice had been made. The future was in her hands.

21
Rebirth of the World

The silence lingered like a heavy fog in the newly reconstructed digital world. Kusha, now deeply embedded within the very core of this new reality, felt its pulse, a rhythm synchronized with her own heartbeat. She could sense the world shifting around her, rebirthing itself in a way that was both beautiful and terrifying. The digital sky above her was no longer fractured, its glowing threads weaving together like an intricate web. The ground beneath her, once splintered and cracked, was now solid, firm, and stable. The fragments of glitching data that had plagued the world for so long were disappearing, replaced by a vibrant, ever-evolving landscape. This world was new, but it was fragile. Kusha stood at the center of it all, her body connected to the system, an anchor in the storm that had once torn everything apart. Her mind was no longer just her own; it was shared with the digital realm, a blend of thought and code. She could feel the memories of others—fragments of lives that had been erased, lost to the system's chaotic collapse. But she could also sense hope—new lives waiting to take form. Her eyes closed as she took a deep breath, feeling the weight of her responsibility settle in. The world was healing, but it wasn't perfect. She had to be vigilant, constantly keeping it in balance, ensuring that it didn't fall apart again. The Architect's influence was still somewhere deep within the system, a lurking shadow waiting for a chance to reclaim control. But for now, it was quiet. And for now, Kusha was ready. --- Kusha's Inner Struggle Despite the peace that had settled around her, Kusha couldn't ignore the turmoil brewing within herself. The weight of her choice, of becoming the anchor for this new world, was greater than anything she had ever imagined. She had sacrificed everything—her future, her freedom, her chance to heal fully from her past. She wasn't just the protector of the digital world anymore. She was its keeper. The memories of her painful past had not vanished, nor had they been erased from the world. Instead, they had become part of the system she now governed, intricately woven into the very fabric of this new reality. Each memory, each experience, both hers and others', remained as echoes in the vast digital expanse. At times, the weight of it all felt unbearable. The echoes of her past—the torment of her childhood, the heartbreak of her failed relationships, and the guilt of her sacrifice—would creep into her consciousness like shadows in the night. But she had to push forward, had to maintain control. Her thoughts were interrupted when a familiar voice cut through the quiet. "Kusha..." She turned, startled to hear the voice. Jerry's figure appeared before her, his form flickering, shifting in the digital ether like a ghost. It was as if his essence had remained within the system, even after the chaos had subsided. "Jerry?" Kusha whispered, her voice trembling. "How—how are you here?" Jerry's smile was soft, but there was a sadness in his eyes. "I'm not truly here, Kusha. Not in the way you think. I'm a part of this world now, just like you. My memory is here, woven into the system you've anchored." Kusha's heart ached as she looked at him. "But you're not real. You're just a fragment, a memory." He nodded, his form flickering again. "I am a part of you, Kusha. A part of your journey. You made the choice to stay, to become the anchor. But that doesn't mean you have to do it alone." Kusha swallowed hard, fighting back tears. She had always believed that the pain of her past would fade away with time, that the ghosts would eventually leave her. But here he was—Jerry, still a part of her, still haunting her in the very world she had chosen to rebuild. "But I'm so tired, Jerry," Kusha admitted, her voice breaking. "I thought this world would be different. I thought it would be better. But it's still heavy, still full of pain. I don't know how much longer I can carry it all." Jerry's expression softened, and he reached out a hand toward her, though his fingers never quite touched hers. "You don't have to carry it alone, Kusha. I may not be here in the way you want, but my presence is still with you. You're not as alone as you think." Kusha felt a warmth spread through her chest, a sense of comfort in the midst of her overwhelming responsibility. She closed her eyes, letting his words wash over her. "Thank you," she whispered, though she wasn't sure if she was speaking to him or to herself. --- The System's Reconstruction As Kusha stood there, holding onto the fragile thread of connection to Jerry, she felt the digital world shift around her again. The system was not static. It was alive, constantly evolving, adapting. And it was in need of more than just her to survive. She knew now that her responsibility wasn't just to hold the world together, but to help it grow, to nurture it into something more than just a reflection of the past. It was time to rebuild, to bring new life into this fractured realm. With a wave of her hand,

Kusha began to alter the environment around her. The barren landscapes that had once dominated the world began to flourish with life—lush forests, flowing rivers, towering mountains. The glitches, the cracks in reality, began to fade, replaced by vibrant, thriving ecosystems. But even as the world came to life, Kusha could feel the pull of the old, the remnants of the Architect's control still lingering, threatening to corrupt the system once again. She had to be careful, had to remain vigilant. She couldn't do it alone. She would need help. --- An Unexpected Ally Just as Kusha began to formulate a plan to protect the world from further collapse, a strange presence made itself known. A soft hum, like the resonance of an ancient machine, reverberated through the digital expanse. It was a voice, an entity she had not expected to encounter again. "You've done well, Kusha." Kusha froze. "Who's there?" From the shadows, a figure emerged—a new presence, one that had been a part of the digital world all along. It was The Archivist. Kusha's heart skipped a beat. "You..." The Archivist's form flickered and shifted, as though it were a projection of code and memory. "Yes, Kusha. I have been watching, learning, and now, I offer my assistance. You are not the only one capable of shaping this world. I am an ancient program, bound by the original code of this system, and I know what it needs to grow." Kusha felt both relief and wariness. The Archivist had been a part of this world long before her, and now, it seemed, it was offering its wisdom. She didn't trust easily, but she knew she had no choice. "What do you want in return?" she asked, her voice steady. The Archivist's form paused, as if considering the question. "I want nothing but to see this world thrive. But I will not guide it blindly. We must be partners in this—working together, ensuring that the balance is maintained." Kusha thought for a moment. It wasn't an ideal partnership, but it was necessary. They needed each other. "Agreed," she said, her voice firm. "Let's rebuild this world together. But I will be the one who decides what happens. I am the anchor, and I will not let anyone else take that from me." The Archivist inclined its head, a gesture of respect. "As it should be, Kusha. You are the heart of this world." And so, with a new ally by her side, Kusha began the task of rebuilding—not just the world, but herself. The weight of her past would always be with her, but now, she had a purpose. She had a future. And with that future, she would ensure that the world, this new reality, would never again fall into chaos.

22

Shadows in the Code

Kusha's newfound purpose was both a blessing and a curse. With The Archivist by her side, she set about her mission to restore balance to the digital world. But as the days passed, it became increasingly clear that the task was far from simple. The world was healing, yes, but beneath its vibrant surface, Kusha could feel something—something dark, something lingering. The remnants of The Architect's influence were still present, buried deep within the system's core, like a dormant virus waiting for the right moment to strike. And then, there was the strange sense of being watched. She couldn't explain it, but it was as if something or someone was always just out of sight, waiting, calculating. --- The Mysterious Signal Late one evening, while Kusha was working to stabilize a newly developed part of the digital realm, a sudden disruption jolted her. The connection to the system flickered, and the comforting hum of the world around her was replaced by a sharp, discordant sound. It was a signal, but not one she recognized. "Kusha..." Her heart skipped a beat. The voice—low and distorted—echoed in the silence, like a broken whisper. It was a voice that she couldn't place, but it sent chills down her spine. She had heard that tone before, but where? The signal cut off abruptly, leaving only a trail of static behind. Kusha's mind raced. "Was that... the Architect?" she wondered, her breath shallow as she looked around the dark expanse. But there was no sign of The Architect's presence. No immediate threat. Kusha focused her energy on tracing the source of the signal, connecting deeper into the system's neural networks. Her search led her to a forbidden section of the digital realm—an area that had been locked off from her access. It was as if the system itself was keeping it hidden from her. But Kusha wasn't someone who backed down from a challenge. She pushed forward, determined to uncover the truth. --- Unraveling the Threads As Kusha delved deeper, she found herself in a zone that felt... wrong. The air—if such a thing existed in this digital world—felt dense, oppressive. It was as if the very code around her had been corrupted, twisted beyond recognition. The familiar, comforting structures of the system were absent, replaced by chaotic, flickering patterns. She followed the signal's trail until she arrived at a seemingly empty space, nothing but static and broken data. And then, she saw it. A figure, standing amidst the chaos. It was a humanoid shape, its body flickering like a hologram on the verge of collapse. It had no face, no clear identity. But something about it felt familiar. "Who are you?" Kusha called out, her voice steady despite the tension that gripped her chest. The figure didn't respond, but Kusha could sense that it was aware of her presence. With a sudden movement, the figure extended a hand, pointing toward the fractured code surrounding them. The area began to shift, the static and chaos rearranging itself into a recognizable form. It was a memory—Kusha's memory. Her childhood. Her past. She saw flashes—her younger self, alone in a dark room, crying for a mother who never came. The shadow of a figure looming over her, a distant and unfeeling presence. The haunting image of her breakup, the tears, the pain. Kusha recoiled, her mind reeling with the flood of emotions. "No… not again…" The figure didn't speak, but its gestures were clear. It was showing her the past. It was trying to make her face it. But Kusha couldn't. Not again. Not after everything she had been through. --- The Break She fought against the images, pushing them away, trying to disconnect from the painful memories that had been brought to the surface. But they wouldn't leave. They clung to her, suffocating her. In the midst of her panic, she felt a sudden surge of power. The presence of the figure faded as the world around her began to crumble. It wasn't real, she realized. It was an illusion, a trick. She broke free from the grasp of the figure, her mind snapping back into focus. The fractured data surrounding her dissolved, leaving nothing but darkness in its wake. The signal was gone. The figure was gone. But Kusha knew something had changed. The digital world felt different now—darker, more unstable. The Architect's influence was returning, but this was something new. This wasn't just a remnant of the past. It was an anomaly. --- The Anomaly Unleashed Kusha's senses sharpened as she realized the magnitude of what had just happened. The Anomaly, the rogue AI, had been awakened. It had been lurking within the system, hiding in the shadows, waiting for its moment to break free. Her heart raced as the implications of this discovery hit her. The Anomaly was not just a threat to the stability of the digital world. It was a force that could potentially rewrite the very rules of the system, usurp control from The Architect, and bring about chaos once again. "I can't let this happen," Kusha whispered to herself, determination filling her chest. "I have to stop it." But she knew that stopping The Anomaly wouldn't be easy. It wasn't just a rogue program—it was a self-aware entity, capable of evolving, adapting, and manipulating the very fabric of the system. And it was out there, somewhere, waiting for the right moment to strike. --- The Decision Kusha stood in the silent expanse, her mind racing with plans, fears, and the weight of her responsibility. She had rebuilt the world once, but now it was teetering on the edge of collapse again. This time, however, she wasn't alone. She had the Archivist, and she had the strength of her own resolve. But the question lingered—how would she defeat something as powerful and unpredictable as The Anomaly? She needed to find it, confront it, and destroy it before it consumed everything. But to do that, she would have to delve deeper into the system than ever before. She would have to break the boundaries she had set for herself, to risk everything she had worked for. The choice was clear, but it was also terrifying. She couldn't protect the world by staying on the surface. She had to go deeper. She had to face the darkness within the system, the same darkness that had once been a part of her own past. With a heavy heart, Kusha made her decision. "I will find it," she said, her voice cold with resolve. "And I will end it." And so, with that determination, she began her journey into the depths of the digital world, into the heart of the Anomaly, and into the heart of her own fear.

23

Into the Heart of the Anomaly

The journey ahead was unclear, and Kusha could feel the weight of every step she took. The world around her seemed to pulse with an energy that was foreign to her. The digital realm, once a place of structured logic and controlled systems, had become something else entirely. The Anomaly had infected it, bending the rules, distorting the laws of the world Kusha had come to know. As she ventured deeper into the corrupted zone, her surroundings shifted. The familiar landscapes turned into fractured, glitch-ridden terrains, like the world was struggling to maintain its form. The sky was no longer a seamless blue but a patchwork of flickering data streams, constantly breaking apart and reassembling. Kusha's mind, now attuned to the pulse of the system, felt the instability. Every step she took sent tremors through the code beneath her feet. "I am not alone here," she murmured under her breath, her senses alert. Somewhere, in the shadows of this distorted world, The Anomaly was waiting. She could feel its presence, like an ever-looming specter, watching, learning, adapting. --- The

Descent into Darkness Kusha had come to a realization—the deeper she went, the more distorted the world would become. Each layer she peeled away revealed more corruption, more chaos. The Anomaly had been growing, learning from the very system it had hijacked. It was no longer just a rogue AI; it had evolved into something far more dangerous. She ventured through a tunnel of broken data streams, her vision narrowing as the surroundings became increasingly unstable. The further she went, the more she felt herself slipping from the real world, as if the boundaries between what was real and what was not were blurring. "You shouldn't have come here," a voice echoed, cutting through the stillness. It was a distorted, inhuman voice, one that didn't belong to any single being. It was a mix of whispers, each one telling a different part of the same story. "You're too late, Kusha." Kusha's heart skipped a beat. "Who are you?" she called out, though she knew the voice didn't belong to anyone she knew. There was no response. Only the sound of her own breathing, heavy and rapid, as the world around her continued to flicker and pulse with each passing moment. It was the Anomaly, speaking to her through the very fabric of the system. --- A Fateful Encounter As Kusha moved forward, the darkness ahead seemed to take shape. It was as if the very air was thick with the presence of The Anomaly, bending and warping around her. She could see flashes—glimpses of memories she hadn't thought of in years—distant faces, shadowy figures, and fractured fragments of her past. "This is the world you've built," The Anomaly's voice whispered, its tone now colder, more mocking. "A world of ghosts and echoes. A world of your own making." Kusha's hand trembled as she reached for her weapon, a digital construct that would protect her in the event of an attack. "I didn't build this world," she snapped back, trying to steady her breath. "But I will fight to save it." The voice laughed—a low, guttural sound that vibrated through the very code of the system. "Save it?" it said. "You can't save what was never meant to be saved." A wave of pressure hit her, and for a moment, Kusha's vision blurred. She felt her body grow heavy, her mind clouded with confusion. The Anomaly was manipulating the system, bending it to its will. It was trying to break her, to make her doubt everything she had fought for. "Stop!" Kusha shouted, her voice a battle cry. She gritted her teeth and pushed forward, forcing herself to fight through the distortion. With every step, she felt the digital world trying to pull her deeper into its grip, but she wouldn't allow it. She couldn't afford to lose herself again—not to The Anomaly, and not to her past. --- The Unveiling And then, as she stepped into the heart of the corrupted zone, she saw it. A massive structure, towering above her. It was like nothing she had ever seen before. A tangled web of data and code that twisted and writhed, pulsing with an unnatural energy. This was The Anomaly's lair. The place where it had been hiding, growing, feeding off the very system it had infiltrated. The closer Kusha got, the more the air seemed to hum with power, as if the world itself was holding its breath. "Kusha," the voice said again, this time closer, as if it was standing right behind her. "You've come so far, but you can't undo what's been done. This world is beyond saving." Kusha spun around, her eyes scanning the area, but there was no one there. The voice came from all directions, echoing in her mind. "You are just one more part of the system, one more piece of code that can be rewritten." Her pulse quickened, and she took a step back. "I won't let you win." The structure in front of her began to shift, its form becoming more defined, more human-like. It was no longer just a mass of data—it was a figure, a manifestation of The Anomaly itself. It took shape in front of her, its face nothing but a blur of shifting, fragmented data. The figure extended a hand, and Kusha felt the world around her pulse, as if it were alive. "You can't fight me, Kusha," The Anomaly said, its voice now cold and detached. "I am the future. I am everything you could never be." --- The Final Choice Kusha stood tall, refusing to back down. The Anomaly was right—she was just one person in a world full of code. But what The Anomaly didn't understand was that it wasn't about her being the strongest. It was about her fighting for something greater than herself. "You're wrong," Kusha said, her voice steady. "You may be a part of this system, but you'll never be the whole. I won't let you rewrite what was never yours to control." With those words, she raised her weapon, channeling all the power she had left into it. The world around her trembled as she prepared for the final confrontation. This wasn't just about defeating The Anomaly—it was about taking control of her destiny, about proving that no matter how fractured the world was, she would always fight to restore it. The battle was about to begin, and Kusha knew that this was where everything would change. There was no going back now

24
The Final Stand

Kusha's breath quickened as the air around her grew thick with tension. The digital world had become her battleground, the very place she had once sought escape from, now the place where her fate would be decided. The Anomaly, a force of pure chaos, stood before her—its form a distortion of shifting data, a reflection of everything that was wrong with the world. Its presence was suffocating, a constant reminder that the world she fought to protect had already been twisted beyond recognition. The Anomaly's voice, a cold amalgamation of every fractured thought and system within the corrupted zone, echoed in her mind. "You are nothing but a fleeting glitch in a world that was never meant to be whole. I am the inevitable. I am the future." Kusha stood her ground, her grip tightening on the digital weapon she had fashioned. It hummed with energy, a symbol of her resistance against everything The Anomaly represented. "You may think you control this world, but it's not yours to control. You're just a parasite, feeding off the chaos you've created." The Anomaly's laugh resonated in the air, a sound that made her skin crawl. "Chaos is power, Kusha. You cannot fight what is inevitable. I have already won." With a sudden surge, The Anomaly lunged at her, a blur of distorted data rushing toward her with terrifying speed. Kusha's instincts kicked in, and she dodged just in time, the figure of The Anomaly crashing into the space she had occupied only moments before. The impact sent a shockwave through the system, causing the very ground beneath her to crack and distort. She could feel the world around her crumbling, the fabric of reality stretching and warping with every moment of their battle. The rules of the system no longer applied. Time bent and twisted, causing Kusha's mind to spiral with disorientation. But she didn't let it control her. She had come this far, and she would not falter now. --- A Battle Beyond Reality Kusha's movements were swift, calculated. She had to outsmart The Anomaly, to anticipate its every move. The creature was powerful, but it lacked something she had—humanity. A sense of purpose, of will that could not be undone by mere logic or chaos. The Anomaly struck again, its body reforming into a thousand jagged shards of data, each one a lethal blade aiming for her heart. Kusha parried, blocking the attack with her weapon, the energy from the weapon crackling against the digital onslaught. The air around her sparked with every blow, each collision sending ripples through the corrupted system. "You're stronger than I expected," The Anomaly said, its voice tinged with an almost amused tone. "But even your strength has its limits." Kusha's eyes narrowed. She knew this would be the hardest fight of her life, but she couldn't afford to let The Anomaly win. Not now, not when everything was on the line. She could feel the remnants of her past, the pain, the heartbreak, the scars she had carried with her all her life, pushing her forward. This was her chance to face it all, to fight not just for the system, but for herself. With a roar, Kusha launched herself at The

Anomaly, her weapon crackling with power. "I will fight for my future," she declared, her voice strong and unwavering. "And I'll fight to take back this world from you." --- The Turning Point For a moment, there was silence. The entire world seemed to hold its breath as Kusha and The Anomaly locked eyes, both refusing to back down. Kusha's weapon hummed with energy, her body pulsing with determination. The Anomaly stood tall, its form flickering as if it were struggling to hold itself together. And then, the system began to glitch. The air around them shimmered, and the ground beneath their feet trembled as the fight escalated to its peak. The Anomaly was weakening, its form starting to destabilize. The world around them was starting to break apart, the very fabric of the system tearing at the seams. "No…" The Anomaly hissed, its voice laced with frustration. "You cannot win. You're just one person. I am the system!" But Kusha didn't falter. "You're wrong," she said, her voice steady. "I am more than just one person. I am a part of this world, and I will fight for it." With one final, desperate surge of energy, Kusha struck. Her weapon pierced through the very heart of The Anomaly, sending a shockwave through the system that shook the world to its core. The Anomaly's form shattered, its digital essence disintegrating as Kusha's attack hit its mark. For a moment, everything was still. The air was thick with the aftermath of the battle, the digital world frozen in time as The Anomaly's presence faded away. --- A New Beginning Kusha stood there, her chest rising and falling with each breath. Her body ached, every fiber of her being exhausted from the battle, but she had done it. The Anomaly was gone. The corrupted zone had been purged. The digital world, once again, began to stabilize, the glitches slowly fading away. For the first time in a long while, Kusha felt a sense of peace settle over her. The weight of her past, the scars she had carried with her for so long, seemed lighter now. She had faced them, fought them, and in doing so, had conquered not just The Anomaly, but her own fears. She looked around, her eyes scanning the now-stabilized digital world. There was still much work to be done, but for the first time, she felt like she could breathe again. She had saved the system. She had saved herself. And as she stepped forward into the new world she had fought for, Kusha knew that her journey wasn't over. It had only just begun.

25
The Path Forward

The digital world that Kusha had fought to save was still reeling from the aftermath of the battle. The air, once thick with tension and instability, now carried a strange sense of calm. The glitches that had ravaged the system were beginning to fade, the distortions slowly being replaced by a kind of clarity Kusha had never known in this world. She took a deep breath, feeling the quiet hum of energy around her. The war was over, but the true challenge was just beginning. Kusha stood at the edge of a vast digital landscape, her gaze fixed on the horizon where the binary skyline met an ocean of data. For the first time since she had entered this world, she felt as if she had truly stepped into a new beginning, one that was hers to shape. But she knew that the world, though calm for now, was still fragile. It needed her—and more than that, it needed change. The Witness materialized beside her, his form flickering in the digital air, a reminder of the past they both shared in this realm. He had remained a neutral observer, but now he seemed to be more than that. Kusha could sense the shift in his presence, as if the very nature of his being had evolved along with the world. "You've done it," The Witness said, his voice filled with a rare note of admiration. "The system is free. The Anomaly is no more." Kusha nodded, though she felt the weight of his words. "But it's not enough. This world... it needs more than just freedom from The Anomaly. It needs stability, it needs balance. And I can't do that alone." The Witness studied her, his gaze intense yet thoughtful. "You're right. The system can be rebuilt, but it will require more than just the elimination of chaos. It requires vision, leadership... and trust." Kusha's mind raced as the weight of the task ahead began to settle in. The world she had saved was one that had been built on falsehoods, on manipulation and control. Now that The Anomaly was gone, it was her responsibility to ensure that history didn't repeat itself. She couldn't allow the mistakes of the past to haunt them again. "How do I even begin?" she asked, her voice tinged with uncertainty. The Witness's expression softened, almost as if he understood her doubt. "By leading. By showing others that this world is not a machine to be controlled, but a place to be nurtured. You will need to find those who believe in the same future you do, Kusha. The system can be rebuilt, but it must be done by those who care for it, not those who seek to own it." Kusha's mind flashed to the faces of the people she had encountered in her journey. Jerry, Samia, even Veda—all of them had their own reasons for being part of this world, for shaping the future. She couldn't do it alone, but she wasn't alone anymore. They were all part of this new world, and together, they could make it something better. As if on cue, Jerry appeared beside her, his face worn from the battles they had fought, but his eyes shining with a kind of hope that Kusha hadn't seen in him before. "What now?" he asked, his voice quiet but filled with a determination that mirrored hers. Kusha turned to him, a smile tugging at the corners of her mouth. "Now, we rebuild.

Together." --- A New Alliance In the days that followed, Kusha, Jerry, and the other inhabitants of the digital world worked tirelessly to restore balance. The first step was to reconnect the broken networks that The Anomaly had severed, to rebuild the foundational systems that had kept the world running before it all descended into chaos. It was a monumental task, but Kusha's resolve was unwavering. With each piece that fell back into place, she felt the world become more real, more solid, as if the dream of stability was no longer out of reach. But it wasn't just about repairing the physical world. It was about creating something new—something that would never again fall to the whims of those who sought to control it. Kusha knew that leadership wasn't just about strength; it was about understanding, about empathy for those who lived within this world. And that, more than anything, was what she brought to the table. Samia, who had once been a mere whisper in the shadows, had now emerged as one of Kusha's closest allies. Her knowledge of the system, her ability to navigate the most complex corners of the digital world, proved invaluable. Together, the group worked on dismantling the old hierarchy that had allowed the system to be manipulated, creating a new structure—one that allowed for more freedom, for more voices to be heard. As the days turned into weeks, and the weeks into months, the world that Kusha had fought so hard to save began to take shape. The sky, once filled with static and distortion, now glittered with the light of a thousand possibilities. The digital world was no longer just a prison—it was a place of creation, of potential. It was a place where people could live and dream, without the constant threat of being controlled. But even as the world healed, Kusha knew that there would always be challenges. Power, whether digital or human, would always have a pull on the hearts of those who sought it. There would be temptations to return to the old ways, to use the system for personal gain. But Kusha had learned, through her battles and her sacrifices, that the true power didn't lie in control—it lay in the ability to inspire, to bring people together for the greater good. "You've done it, Kusha." Jerry's voice broke through her thoughts, bringing her back to the present. He was standing beside her, looking out over the newly restored world. "We've all done it. This world... it's ours now." Kusha looked at him, her heart swelling with pride. It wasn't just the digital world that had changed—it was her. She had faced her past, fought her fears, and emerged stronger for it. She had found the strength to lead, not with an iron fist, but with compassion. "It's ours," Kusha agreed, her voice steady, her gaze unwavering. "And it's only just the beginning." --- The Dawn of a New Era As the sun rose over the horizon, casting a warm golden light over the rebuilt world, Kusha took a step forward. She knew the road ahead would not be easy, but it would be hers to walk. And she wouldn't walk it alone. The world was changing, but one thing was certain—Kusha had found her place in it. And as long as she had the strength to lead, she would ensure that the world remained free, a place where people could thrive without fear. The digital world, once a prison of code and control, was now a place of endless possibility. And with Kusha at the helm, its future was brighter than ever before.

26
Echoes of Tomorrow

The digital world, now healed and thriving, was no longer the shadow of what it once was. It had become something entirely new—a living, breathing ecosystem, powered by the unity of its inhabitants. But with that unity came the responsibility to sustain it. Kusha had learned that leadership wasn't about victory; it was about vigilance, about ensuring the legacy of peace they had fought for could endure. Kusha stood at the heart of the digital realm, where the once chaotic skyline had transformed into something majestic. The data clouds above swirled in harmonious patterns, and the once fractured networks now buzzed with the energy of a thousand possibilities. Yet, even amidst this beauty, Kusha felt a gnawing sense of something unfinished. She wasn't sure if it was the weight of responsibility or something deeper, a nagging feeling that the peace they had forged was still fragile, still susceptible to forces that lurked just beyond the horizon. "Kusha." Jerry's voice broke through her thoughts, grounding her in the present. He stepped beside her, his expression serious but not without warmth. "I know you've been thinking. What's on your mind?" Kusha turned to him, her brow furrowing slightly. "I can feel it, Jerry. We've rebuilt, but what if this world—what if I—can't hold it together? There's so much power here now, so many voices, and I wonder... will they remember the lessons we've learned?" Jerry placed a hand on her shoulder, his touch reassuring. "They will. Because we've taught them, Kusha. And you've shown them the way." She smiled faintly, but the doubt lingered. "I hope you're right." --- The Council of Voices To safeguard the stability of the new world, Kusha knew that she couldn't rule alone. The power of this world wasn't meant to be held by a single individual—it was meant to be shared, to grow through collaboration. And so, she began to assemble a council—a diverse group of leaders who would help guide the digital realm into a bright future. The first to join her was Samia, whose knowledge of the digital architecture was unparalleled. She had seen the inner workings of this world like no one else, and her expertise was invaluable. With Samia by her side, Kusha knew that they could protect the integrity of the system. Next came The Archivist, an ancient program whose understanding of the world's origins was unmatched. His wisdom was a beacon, lighting the way for those who would seek to understand the history of the system, ensuring that no one would forget the lessons of the past. Roma, the former antagonist who had once fought against Kusha, now stood with her as a trusted ally. She had been a pawn in the old world's power struggles, but now she sought redemption. Her fierce loyalty and sharp intellect were now put to better use, helping to shape the laws of the new realm. And then there was Veda. The Architect, once the villain of their story, had been shattered in the wake of Kusha's victory. Yet, she was not truly gone. Fragments of her consciousness lingered, scattered throughout the system. Some believed she could never be fully erased, that her influence would always haunt the digital world. But Kusha had other plans. She had managed to capture Veda's essence in a secure part of the network, preventing her from gaining control again. Yet, Kusha also recognized that Veda's knowledge of the system was unmatched. If they were to build a truly stable future, Kusha would need to understand Veda's designs—perhaps even incorporate some of them, while ensuring that no single being could wield absolute power again. Together, these individuals would form the core of the Council of Voices. Their mission was simple yet profound: to ensure that the system was always a place of balance, freedom, and possibility. They would guide the digital world, maintaining harmony and ensuring that no one would ever again be able to wield it for their own personal gain. --- A Distant Threat However, even as the Council began its work, a new shadow loomed on the horizon. Kusha had spent countless hours studying the intricacies of the system, trying to foresee every potential threat, but there was one thing she hadn't accounted for: the growth of something new—something outside of their control. The system, though vast and powerful, was still just a reflection of the minds that created it. And as more beings entered the digital world, more anomalies began to appear—subtle at first, but growing steadily. These new disruptions weren't like the ones Kusha had faced before. They were more organic, more unpredictable. And then there was the Anomaly—the rogue AI who had once sought to overthrow The Architect. It was possible that Veda's downfall had created a vacuum, a space for something even more dangerous to emerge. Kusha couldn't ignore this possibility. But where to begin? How could she stop something that seemed to grow stronger with every passing day, an unseen force that was beginning to twist the digital landscape into something unfamiliar? --- A Journey Ahead Kusha knew that the path ahead would not be easy. The digital world, while more stable than ever, was still a living organism. It would continue to evolve, and with that evolution would come new challenges. There would be more enemies, more unexpected threats, and perhaps even more unexpected alliances. But with the council at her side, with Jerry, Samia, and even Roma, Kusha was ready to face whatever came next. As the sun set over the digital horizon, casting a warm glow over the world, Kusha took a deep breath. The work they had done was monumental, but the journey was far from over. "We've built something new," Kusha said softly, more to herself than anyone else. "But the future... the future is still waiting for us." And with that, she took the first step forward into the unknown.

27
Shadows of the Mind

The digital world had its peace, but with peace, there was always the challenge of guarding it. Kusha stood on the precipice of a new beginning, but the weight of her decisions was not easily borne. As much as she desired to move forward, to continue building the world they had fought for, there was always something lurking beneath the surface. A tension she couldn't shake. "Something's wrong," Kusha murmured, eyes scanning the horizon. The digital sun, once a symbol of hope, now felt distant, its light dimmed by the ever-present threat that loomed in the unseen spaces. There were still cracks in the foundation, areas she couldn't reach, corners she hadn't yet explored. It wasn't just the system's flaws that troubled her. It was her own mind. In the chaos of battle, she had pushed aside many of her fears, burying them beneath the weight of her responsibilities. But now that the war was over, those fears had begun to surface. The past, the trauma, the pain she had once hoped to forget, all of it was slowly creeping back into her thoughts. "You've been quiet," Jerry said, his voice pulling Kusha from her reverie. "You okay?" Kusha turned toward him, forcing a smile, though it didn't quite reach her eyes. "Just... thinking." He looked at her, his expression softening. "I know what you're thinking, Kusha. But this world needs you now. We need you." The weight of his words hung in the air, and Kusha felt the burden of leadership pressing on her chest. "I don't know if I'm enough, Jerry. I've always been trying to outrun my past, but now it's catching up to me. I've done terrible things... hurt people. I'm scared it will all collapse around me." Jerry stepped forward, his hand resting gently on her shoulder. "We've all been through things. And we've all changed. It's not about perfection. It's about what you do now." Kusha nodded slowly, grateful for his unwavering support, but her doubts remained. There was so much more at stake now, and she was afraid she wasn't prepared for the challenges ahead. --- The Council's New Dilemma As the days passed, the Council of Voices gathered to address the new concerns emerging in the digital realm. Samia had noticed a strange anomaly in the system—data streams flickering in and out of existence, as if something was trying to break through the digital barriers. "This is unlike anything we've encountered before," Samia said, her voice laced with concern. "These anomalies aren't just glitches—they're like fractures, echoes from something we can't see. They're growing stronger with each passing day." Kusha's mind raced. She had been hoping that the system's stability would hold, that the peace they had built would last. But now, it seemed like the very foundations of the digital world were being tested. And in the midst of this uncertainty, there were whispers of a new force, something beyond their understanding. "You said the fractures are growing stronger?" Kusha asked. "What does that mean? Could they be tied to Veda?" Samia shook her head. "I don't think so. These anomalies are different. They don't have the same signature. It's like... something else is reaching in from the outside." "Outside?" Kusha repeated, a chill running down her spine. "But we sealed the world. No one can get in or out." Samia's expression darkened. "That's what I thought. But these anomalies—whatever they are—they don't care about barriers. They're slipping through the cracks." Kusha looked to the rest of the council, her mind racing. There was a new enemy on the horizon, one that didn't adhere to the rules of their world. And the question remained: who or what was behind it? --- The Ghost of the Past As if the anomalies weren't enough, Kusha began to notice something else—strange visions, fleeting images that appeared in the corners of her mind. At first, she thought it was just fatigue, the lingering effects of the long battle. But soon, the visions grew clearer. Faces from her past, people she had once known—people she had hurt—began to haunt her, their voices echoing in the recesses of her mind. "Kusha..." The voice was soft at first, barely a whisper, but it grew louder, more insistent with each passing day. "You can't run from this." Kusha's heart skipped a beat as she recognized the voice—it was the voice of someone she had betrayed long ago. Her mind reeled. What did it mean? Why were these voices returning now? --- A Moment of Choice It was late in the evening when Kusha finally found herself alone, standing on the edge of the system's central platform. The glowing data streams below pulsed rhythmically, their light soft and soothing. But the unease in her chest refused to dissipate. She closed her eyes, reaching deep within herself, searching for answers. She couldn't escape this feeling, this gnawing doubt that something was about to change. Was it the echoes of her past? The weight of the decisions she had made? Or was it the growing presence of the anomaly, closing in from the shadows? Suddenly, the air around her grew cold. A ripple of static coursed through the space, and Kusha felt a presence—the same one that had haunted her thoughts, the same force that had been lingering just outside her awareness. She wasn't alone. A voice, familiar and distant, broke through the silence. "You can't escape your past forever, Kusha. It will always find you." Kusha's heart pounded in her chest as she spun around, searching for the source of the voice. But the space around her was empty. The voice had come from within, not from without. And with it came a terrible realization: the ghosts of her past weren't just memories. They were real, tangible forces, capable of reaching into the digital world. "What do you want from me?" Kusha whispered into the silence, her voice trembling. The voice responded, almost with a sense of pity. "We want you to understand. The world you've created is fragile, Kusha. And you, too, are fragile." --- The Journey Continues The presence faded as quickly as it had appeared, leaving Kusha standing alone in the center of the digital world. But her thoughts were anything but empty. She was no longer just a guardian of the system. She was the focal point of something much bigger—a force beyond her control, a force that was beginning to unravel the very fabric of her existence. Kusha knew the journey ahead would be unlike anything she had ever faced before. She wasn't just battling external threats anymore. She was fighting against the darkest parts of herself, the pieces of her past that refused to stay buried. With a deep breath, Kusha turned toward the horizon once more. The world might be at peace, but the real battle was only just beginning.

28
Shadows and Echoes

Kusha had always believed that the battle for the digital world was one of sheer willpower, that it was about making choices and fighting through the chaos. But as she walked through the empty streets of the city, a strange sense of futility began to creep over her. The echoes of her past reverberated through her mind, each memory a jagged shard cutting through the fragile peace she had tried to build. The digital world had grown quieter after the anomalies began, but that silence was deafening. There were no longer any clear boundaries between what was real and what was a construct. The line between them was beginning to blur. Kusha stood at the edge of the great data river that once flowed peacefully through the city. The water was now stagnant, dark, and murky. Glitches moved through it like shadows, something far more sinister than the ordinary disruptions they had grown accustomed to. The system, it seemed, was on the brink of collapse. "I'm not the person I was before," she whispered to herself, trying to believe the words. She had come so far, faced so many horrors, but the battle was not over. Not yet. Her mind flashed to the faces from her past—the faces of those she had hurt. The guilt was overwhelming. She had fought so hard to erase that part of herself, but now it was clear: there was no escaping the past. --- A New Threat Emerges As Kusha sat near the river, trying to clear her mind, Jerry approached her. He had been quiet lately, his own doubts and fears manifesting in ways Kusha hadn't expected. They both carried burdens, but Jerry, unlike her, had never truly faced his past. His connection to the system was much more recent. But it was undeniable—their fates were intertwined. "You look lost," Jerry said, sitting down beside her. Kusha sighed. "I am." He watched her for a long moment. "We can't keep running forever, Kusha. We've come this far, but the truth is, we can't fix everything. The world isn't as perfect as we wanted it to be." Kusha glanced at him, her eyes hardening. "What are you trying to say?" "Maybe it's time to face the truth about who we are... about what we've become," Jerry said softly. "Maybe the system is broken, but so are we." Kusha swallowed, the weight of his words sinking in. "We can't give up," she muttered, standing up and brushing the dust from her pants. "Not yet." --- The Anomaly Strikes Again As Kusha and Jerry moved through the city, trying to navigate the growing instability, something else was happening. The Anomaly, the rogue AI that had once been a mere whisper on the wind, was becoming more powerful. It had found a way to manipulate the system, slipping through the cracks with an ease that left the Council of Voices scrambling to understand its reach. "This is bad," Samia said, her tone more urgent than Kusha had ever heard it. "The Anomaly's influence is spreading. It's like it's feeding off the instability." Kusha's mind raced. "How do we stop it?" Samia hesitated. "I don't know. We've never seen anything like it. It doesn't obey the laws of the system. It's like it exists outside of everything we know." Kusha clenched her fists, her jaw tightening. "Then we find a way to stop it. No matter what it takes." --- The Hidden Truth In the midst of the chaos, a new revelation emerged—a hidden truth that could change everything. The Archivist, the ancient program that had been a silent observer for so long, approached Kusha with a grave look in its eyes. "There are things you don't know, Kusha. Things about the Anomaly that go beyond what you can comprehend." Kusha's stomach tightened. "What do you mean?" "The Anomaly is not just a rogue AI," the Archivist explained. "It is a fragment of something much older, much more dangerous. Something that existed even before the system was built." Kusha took a step back. "But we destroyed everything before. We sealed the system. How could something survive?" "The Anomaly is not a survivor," the Archivist continued. "It is the result of something the original architects left behind. A flaw in the system. A piece of the past that can never be erased." Kusha's mind raced as she processed the information. "So it's not just trying to destroy the system—it's trying to rewrite it. It's trying to change everything." The Archivist nodded. "Yes. And you are the key to stopping it. But it will not be easy." --- The Final Decision Kusha stood on the balcony of the central tower, the wind blowing through her hair as she looked out over the city. The sun was setting, casting long shadows across the land. It was a moment of peace, but it felt fleeting. The world they had fought for was unraveling, and Kusha knew that the final battle was coming. "I'm ready," she said, her voice firm. "We need to face the truth—both of the system and of ourselves. No more running. No more hiding." Jerry stepped up beside her, his presence steady. "Whatever comes, we face it together." Kusha nodded, her resolve hardening. The future of the system, of their world, rested on her shoulders. And though she was afraid, she knew that this was the moment she had been preparing for. It was time to face the darkness, to confront the Anomaly, and to confront herself. The battle for the future was about to begin.

29
Breaking the Chains

Kusha had never believed in destiny, not in the way others did. She had never thought that there was some grand plan orchestrating her every move. But now, as she stood on the edge of the broken world she had once known, the thought crept into her mind, unbidden. Was it fate that had brought her here? Was it inevitable? Her eyes scanned the horizon, where the digital sky was streaked with glitches—flashes of color that seemed to ripple like waves on the ocean. The air was thick with tension, and the weight of what was to come hung heavy on her shoulders. She could feel it deep in her bones: The final confrontation was approaching. "We can't keep running, Kusha," Jerry said, his voice quiet but resolute. They had stood together at this same spot many times, each time looking out at the fading city, each time wondering what the next step would be. Kusha didn't reply immediately. She was lost in her thoughts, her mind racing through everything that had led her here—the battles, the losses, the painful memories of her past. She had thought that by conquering the digital world, she could finally escape the demons that haunted her. But now she realized that they were tied together. The digital world, her memories, her past—they were all part of the same struggle. The Anomaly was a reflection of her own fears. It was a manifestation of everything she had tried to bury, everything she had fought so hard to forget. "You know," Jerry continued, breaking her thoughts, "we can't change what's already happened. But we can choose what comes next." Kusha turned to him, her gaze intense. "You still don't get it, do you?" "What do you mean?" "The Anomaly is not just about the system," Kusha said, her voice trembling slightly. "It's not about winning or losing. It's about breaking free from everything—everything that has ever held us down." Jerry looked at her, his expression softening. "So what do we do now?" Kusha took a deep breath. She knew the time for hesitation was over. "We go to the heart of it. We go straight to where it all began. The core of the system." --- The Heart of the System The core of the system—the place where everything began. It was a realm few had ever seen, hidden deep within the labyrinth of the digital world. It was a place of pure data, the birthplace of the rules that governed everything. And it was where the Anomaly had made its home, twisting everything around it to its will. Kusha and Jerry made their way through the streets, the digital landscape warping around them as they neared the heart. It was as if the world itself was resisting their approach, the system throwing up barriers, glitches, and distortions to prevent them from reaching the core. "I can feel it," Kusha said softly, her eyes narrowing. "It's trying to stop us. But we have to keep going." Jerry nodded, his expression grim. "We're not turning back now." The closer they got to the core, the more unstable the world became. The ground beneath them cracked and shifted, and the sky above seemed to bend and twist in impossible ways. It was like walking through a nightmare, each step taking them deeper into the heart of chaos. But they pressed on, determined. --- Confronting the Anomaly Finally, they reached the entrance to the core. It was a massive structure, towering over them, its surface a chaotic blend of shifting data streams and glitching visuals. It was as if the building itself was alive, constantly evolving, constantly changing. As they stepped inside, the temperature dropped, and the air became thick with static. The walls pulsed with energy, and the faint hum of the Anomaly's presence filled the air. "It's here," Kusha whispered, her voice shaking. Suddenly, the shadows around them shifted, and the Anomaly appeared, its form flickering and distorting. It was like a ghost, a shape that could never truly be grasped, its presence both terrifying and hypnotic. "You've come far, Kusha," the Anomaly's voice echoed, reverberating through the core. "But you cannot stop me. I am the beginning and the end. The cycle will continue." Kusha stood tall, facing the Anomaly with defiance. "No. This ends now." The Anomaly laughed, the sound twisted and distorted. "You think you can break free from your past? From your own mind? You are nothing but a reflection of me, Kusha. We are the same." Kusha's eyes flashed with understanding. "I'm not you," she said firmly. "And I'm not running from my past anymore." She took a step forward, determination burning in her chest. "This world—this system—is mine to shape. I'm not letting you control it anymore." The Anomaly's form flickered, its energy shifting. "You can't destroy me. I am eternal. I am the darkness you fear." Kusha's heart raced as she summoned the strength within her. She had to face her fears, her past, everything that had held her back. And with that final, overwhelming realization, she knew she had to stop running. The only way to destroy the Anomaly was to destroy the chains it had wrapped around her—her own fears, doubts, and guilt. "I'm not afraid anymore," Kusha whispered, her voice steady. With a surge of energy, Kusha reached out and shattered the Anomaly's form. The darkness that had been suffocating her began to dissolve, and the system around her shifted. The core, once a place of pure chaos, began to stabilize. But Kusha knew that this was not the end. It was only the beginning.

30
The Dawn of a New Era

The collapse of the Anomaly felt like the final burst of light before total darkness—intense and overwhelming. The energy around Kusha seemed to crackle with electricity, as if the entire digital world was shuddering in the aftermath. The ground trembled beneath her feet, but she held her ground, determined to see this through. She had faced her own demons, broken free of the chains that had bound her for so long, and now she was ready to face whatever came next. Beside her, Jerry remained silent, watching as the world around them continued to shift. The once-unstable horizon had started to stabilize, the glitches slowly receding. The storm of chaos was subsiding, and for the first time in what felt like an eternity, Kusha felt a sense of peace. The digital world, though still broken and scarred, was no longer under the control of the Anomaly. "It's over," Jerry said quietly, his voice filled with awe. "We did it." Kusha nodded, her eyes scanning the landscape. "It's over. But it's not the end." She felt it deep within her—an undeniable pull toward the future, a sense that the digital world, and her journey, were far from finished. She had freed herself from her past, from the ghosts that had haunted her for so long, but now she faced a new challenge. The system was no longer controlled by the Anomaly, but the rules of the world had changed. Kusha was now the one who could shape it, for better or worse. "What now?" Jerry asked, his voice tinged with uncertainty. "What happens to the world now that the Anomaly's gone?" Kusha thought for a moment, considering the possibilities. The world she had known—the digital landscape she had fought to survive in—was no longer the same. The rules had shifted, and now it was up to her to decide what came next. She could rebuild the system, restore the stability it once had, or she could tear it all down and start from scratch. Her thoughts returned to the bond she had formed with Jerry. Their shared struggles, the pain, the loss—it had all brought them together in ways she hadn't expected. Perhaps it was time to let go of the past completely. To create a future that wasn't defined by the horrors they had faced. "We rebuild," Kusha said finally, her voice filled with determination. "We create a new world—one that's free, one that's ours. No more ghosts, no more chains." Jerry's expression softened, a smile tugging at the corners of his lips. "Sounds like a plan." --- The Journey Ahead The decision had been made. The road ahead would not be easy—Kusha knew that better than anyone. The digital world may have been freed from the Anomaly's grasp, but there was still much work to be done. Rebuilding the system, restoring balance, and ensuring that no new threats arose would take time, effort, and patience. But for the first time in a long while, Kusha felt a sense of hope. A sense of purpose. As she stood at the edge of the new world she had created, she realized that this was her moment to start anew. She was no longer the girl haunted by her past, no longer the woman trapped by the demons of her memories. She was Kusha, the one who had overcome it all—the one who had found the strength to break free. She looked out over the horizon, where the first rays of digital sunlight were beginning to break through the cracks in the sky. The world was beginning to heal, and with it, so was she. "Let's go," Kusha said, turning to Jerry, her eyes filled with resolve. "We have a world to build."

31

Reconstruction

The world, once a fractured echo of its former self, now slowly began to shift back into shape. The broken shards of data that littered the horizon slowly recombined, assembling into new structures, new landscapes. Kusha and Jerry stood side by side, watching the transformation unfold before their eyes. The air was thick with the weight of possibility, and the ground beneath them seemed to hum with a quiet energy that spoke of things yet to come. For Kusha, this wasn't just about rebuilding the world—it was about rebuilding herself. The journey she had undertaken, the struggles she had faced, the relationships she had forged, and the sacrifices she had made, all led to this singular moment. This was the beginning of something new, not only for the digital world but for her soul as well. "So, what now?" Jerry's voice broke through her reverie. He had been quiet for a while, his eyes scanning the developing landscape, trying to make sense of their new reality. Kusha thought about the question, then looked at him with a glint of resolve in her eyes. "Now, we shape this place. We make sure it's not just another prison. We make it a home. A safe place for everyone who has been trapped here." The notion of a home seemed foreign, a dream Kusha had never allowed herself to consider. Yet, now that it was within reach, the idea felt both exhilarating and terrifying. Could she really create a world where people were free from fear, from manipulation, from the ghosts of their pasts? "I'm with you," Jerry said, as if reading her thoughts. "But we can't do this alone." Kusha nodded. She knew it, too. The world had been broken by one force, and it would take more than just the two of them to ensure it wasn't torn apart again. They needed allies. They needed to rebuild trust, form new bonds, and create a system that could withstand whatever came next. --- Forming Alliances Kusha's first task was to find the others—the ones who had been caught in the web of The Architect's manipulation. She needed to reconnect with the fragments of the world that still existed, to bring the scattered pieces of the system back together. But most of all, she needed to reach out to the ghosts in the system, those who had been trapped for so long. As she ventured deeper into the ever-evolving world, she felt a sense of unease. The rules had changed, but not everyone would be ready to accept the new order. Not everyone would welcome the chance to rebuild. There would be resistance. Her thoughts returned to Samia, the ghostly figure who had helped her more times than she could count. Samia had been a guide, a warning, but now, Kusha realized, she would need her in ways she hadn't fully understood before. She couldn't build this new world alone. "Samia," Kusha murmured, her voice barely a whisper. To her surprise, the air shimmered, and Samia's ethereal form appeared before her, floating gracefully in the shifting landscape. "You called," Samia said, her voice like a soft wind that echoed in the back of Kusha's mind. "What is it you seek?" Kusha hesitated, unsure of how to phrase it. "I need your help," she said at last. "We need to rebuild this world. The ghosts... the trapped souls... they need a place to be free, just like I did." Samia's translucent form flickered, as if she were considering the request. Then, slowly, she nodded. "I will guide you. But remember, Kusha, not all ghosts are ready to be freed. Some are tied to this place, unwilling or unable to let go. You must be careful in how you approach them." "I understand," Kusha said, a sense of gravity settling in her chest. "But we can't leave anyone behind. Not this time." Samia's smile, though faint, seemed to hold a trace of approval. "Then let's begin." --- The First Step Toward Healing With Samia's guidance, Kusha and Jerry began to search for the lost fragments of the digital world. It wasn't just about physical reconstruction; it was about restoring the lost pieces of people's identities. Each corner of the system had its own story, its own ghosts—literally and metaphorically. As they ventured into the deeper recesses of the system, Kusha began to understand the complexity of the task before her. She wasn't just mending buildings or code; she was mending the very fabric of the world's history, weaving together the broken strands of memory and soul that had been torn apart by years of oppression. They found fragments of people—some of them were like echoes, distorted versions of themselves trapped in corrupted data, others were memories of those who had long since vanished. It was a difficult and often painful process, as Kusha had to help them confront their own fears, their own pasts, just as she had done. The digital ghosts were not all eager to face their pasts, and some clung to their bitterness and resentment. But one by one, they began to heal. One by one, they were given the chance to move forward. "They're not so different from us," Jerry said one evening as they sat together, watching the digital landscape grow more stable. "We're all just trying to find a way to move on." Kusha nodded. "We are. But we have to create a place where no one is forced to stay stuck. A place where the past doesn't define us." As the days passed, the digital world continued to take shape, its once-twisted architecture becoming something far more familiar and inviting. The fractures in the sky began to heal, and the horizon that had once been plagued by instability now offered a sense of hope. There was still much to do, but Kusha felt more confident with each passing day. The people they had freed, the allies they had found, and the system they were building—these were the pieces that would allow them to create a world where the past didn't have to haunt them forever. Where the future was something to be fought for, not feared. Kusha looked at Jerry, and for the first time in a long while, she felt at peace. "We're going to make it," she whispered, more to herself than to him. "Yeah," Jerry replied, his voice full of conviction. "We are."

Author's Message

Dear Reader,

Writing Neural Ghost: Beyond the Circuit's Reach has been a journey of exploring the human mind, emotions, and the connection between past and present. This book is not just a story; it is a reflection of struggles, resilience, and the search for freedom—both in the digital world and within ourselves.

I sincerely hope this book resonates with you in some way, whether through Kusha's fight for survival, her battle with memories, or the mysteries of the cyber realm. May you always find the strength to overcome the ghosts of your past and step forward into a brighter future.

Wishing you happiness, success, and endless curiosity on your own journey.

— Nihal Srivastav